HOME CAT BLUES

THE CLEVER CAT MYSTERIES
BOOK 7

ALISON O'LEARY

BLOODHOUND
BOOKS

CHAPTER ONE

H e stared down at the old photograph. The faces of the boys that hadn't quite made it into the first team stared back at him, his own among them. He felt a rush of resentment. It still rankled that he hadn't been picked for the first eleven, even though he was clearly one of the best players in the school. It was a similar story when it came to class prefect and just about anything else that conferred some kind of superiority. It was always the same ones that got picked. The golden boys and girls that got everything handed to them on a plate. He smiled grimly. But not anymore. These days he didn't wait to be picked. He just helped himself.

Jeremy sank down on the sofa and hauled Aubrey onto his lap. He was tired, much more tired than he had thought he would be. As he had walked down the corridor this morning he would have known where he was even if he had his eyes closed. The smell of the school seeped through every wall. It was as familiar as an old raincoat. Eau de Sir Franks. He half smiled to himself.

At one time he would have bet a considerable amount of money that he would never come back, that having escaped to His Majesty's Inspectorate, his days of breaking up classroom fights and checking that his car still had all its tyres before setting off home were well and truly over. And yet there he was. Newly appointed head teacher. There would be some faces that he recognised in the staff meeting, and some new ones too, but whether they were old hands or just starting out, he had known that he had to make the right first impression.

He ran his hand over Aubrey's thick fur, feeling himself relax against the rich warmth. He hadn't anticipated feeling quite so drained. Standing in front of fellow teachers, most if not all of whom expected him to improve their professional lives, had induced in him an unexpected level of stress. It was one thing to address teachers on a one to one basis as an Ofsted inspector, knowing that your paths were unlikely to cross again in the near future. It was quite another to stand in front of a room full of people that you would be seeing day in, day out – week in, week out – and who would quite rightly hold you to account if you didn't at least try to fulfil your promises.

Standing there this afternoon in the staffroom – still furnished with the nineteen-sixties easy chairs and coffee tables that had been installed in that bright new decade of promise and optimism when the school had been built – he had looked at the raised expectant faces of the gathered staff and wondered what madness had possessed him to apply for the job at all. But only briefly.

Jeremy knew very well why he had applied for the post. He had been growing increasingly frustrated with being an inspector. It was all very well in those high achieving schools and colleges where there were lots of positives to observe and comment on, but it was rather less rosy in those institutions that had seemed to merely stagger from one academic year to the next with little or no hope of improving. It had all begun to seem so negative. What every school needed at the helm was an enthusiastic and talented leader who could carry the staff with them, a senior team to help, and an input of pupils who were willing to meet them at least halfway. What a worryingly large number actually had was a head who spent their time either firefighting or hiding in their office and a staff who were counting down the days until they could retire or escape to something else.

Sir Franks fell squarely into the latter category. What it needed now was at the very least a steadying pair of hands, which, without undue modesty, he thought he could provide. He couldn't make things any worse, that was for sure. Besides which, as an inspector he had been mostly working from home, apart from the actual inspection visits, and it had started to pall. Zoom meetings with colleagues were all very well, but what he had missed was the buzz of actually being with other people, the little dramas, the sense of belonging, the catching up with the gossip. All right, he often had a gossip with Aubrey and Vincent but, frankly, they didn't contribute much, so it was all a bit one-sided. And they had a disconcerting habit of washing their ears while he was talking.

One thing you could say about Sir Franks, at least the staff and pupils didn't wash their ears when he talked. It was also true to say that working at Sir Franks was very rarely boring. Stressful, definitely. Chaotic, occasionally. At times, positively frightening. But never boring. When the head teacher's post had come up, it had been irresistible.

He looked up as Molly came in.

"How did it go?"

He smiled at her.

"It was okay." He spoke slowly, reaching for the right word. "Weird, but okay."

"Weird in what way?"

"I've sat in those sorts of meetings countless times, but this time I was the one in charge." He laughed suddenly. "I didn't have the option of sitting at the back and doodling on the agenda or checking my phone."

"Were there many new staff?"

Jeremy nodded.

"A few. Obviously appointed before I started, so I'm going to have to make a point of getting to know them, and then the rest were a roundup of the usual suspects. They seemed pleased to see me anyway."

Which was, he thought, hardly surprising. Given the unmitigated disaster of the last permanent headship, they would probably have welcomed Genghis Khan. Before long term sick leave had been followed by the offer of early retirement – which had been accepted with unseemly haste – the last head had inflicted every initiative she had ever stumbled upon on the long-suffering staff, and then thrown in some of her own for good measure.

The declaration that, in the interest of sustainability, all of Year Ten would learn to make their own clothes, and that one afternoon a week would be devoted to the task, had been nothing short of a Jacobean tragedy. Apart from taking out teaching time in core subjects, which many of the pupils desperately needed, it was a mark of the project's complete lack of success that not one item of clothing was ever finished. It was, however, a credit to the ingenuity of the kids that they were able to be so inventive with needles and scissors. Although, the local A&E department hadn't been quite so impressed.

The end result had been that the sewing machines and fabrics the head had wasted a large chunk of the school budget on were quietly disposed of, and the project was never mentioned again. Since her departure, there had been much debate over whether to close the school altogether, which had resulted in a series of interim head teachers being appointed. They appeared to have done nothing other than to keep the seat warm before making for the exit as soon as their contract would allow. The consequence had been that a great flop of apathy, occasionally punctured by a frenzied outburst of anarchy, had hung over the school.

He was determined to change things, to turn the school around. It would be difficult, but surely it could be done. He'd read about other schools, failing schools in dismal areas where expectations were low and achievement even lower, but where discipline and standards had been imposed with astonishing results. Schools where the head teacher and staff were united in working for change. If they could do it, why couldn't Sir Franks? If he could get at least some of the staff on side, he was sure it could be improved.

He thought about the new members of staff that he'd met today, those untainted by the previous failings of the school. They were, surely, one way forward. Young, apparently keen, they all looked like promising material. During the staff meeting they had sat and listened attentively, pens poised, ready to make notes on their fresh new notepads. They were like almost every new intake of young teachers that he'd seen. But, he reflected, there was one that stood out slightly from the rest. Clarissa Ingram. There was something about her. She wasn't like the others. She had a certain poise about her and she spoke differently. He didn't know much about women's fashion but he'd guess that those weren't chain store clothes she was wearing. If he had to put money on it he would say that she hadn't been state school educated, either. He'd check out her file tomorrow.

CHAPTER TWO

Aubrey and Vincent strolled across the front lawn, luxuriating in the last of the afternoon sun. A faint September tang hung in the air, holding the promise of changing seasons and with it a new start. Jeremy and Molly would be home soon, Jeremy from Sir Franks and Molly from her voluntary work at the hospital.

Aubrey turned to Vincent.

"Who'd have thought it, Vin?"

Vincent nodded, his sleek black fur and bright clear eyes a testament to his restored good health. Aubrey looked at him affectionately. Vincent had given him a scare that last time he was ill. Thank goodness the tablets from the vet had put him right. While they both hated vets with a feline passion, it couldn't be denied that they knew how to mend you when necessary.

"Feels good to be back."

Aubrey agreed. It did feel good to be back. This was home. While he'd enjoyed living at the seaside with all its rock pools and summer visitors – the latter offering seemingly endless food opportunities with their picnics on the beach and half-eaten fish and chips – being back here in their old neighbourhood just felt great. They weren't in the same house they'd lived in before though, which he'd been a bit disappointed about to start with. There were new people living there now. Aubrey had heard Molly telling Jeremy that she hoped that they were nice. Aubrey did, too. He had some good memories of living there. It had been where Jeremy and Molly had brought him back from The Big House, aka Sunny Banks rescue centre. And it was also where they had taken Vincent in after his owners had mysteriously disappeared. He would hate to think of, say, some cat haters living there. But he and Vincent had checked it out shortly after they had arrived back and the house still had the cat flap so either they had a cat of their own or they'd forgotten about it. Anyway, it meant that he and Vincent could get in whenever they felt like it. The house they were living in now wasn't so far away and it would only be a short stroll. It would be something to do when they were bored.

He looked around him approvingly. He'd loved their old house but, once he'd got over his initial disappointment of not going back there, he liked this new house too and so did Vincent. This one had an even bigger garden for them to muck about in and it backed onto fields which opened up all sorts of possibilities. The only blot on the landscape was the reappearance of Rupert and Roger. His heart sunk at the thought of the pair of Siamese who, apparently, were still running the manor. Almost as bad, their nark Lupin was still on the scene. As they'd discovered when his snouty little nose had come sniffing around almost before they'd had time to stake out the possibility of the airing cupboard as sleeping quarters.

On a positive note though, Moses was also still around. His heart lifted again as he thought about his little friend. Taking the words intellectual and challenged to whole new heights, but affectionate and loyal with a heart as big as a lion's, Moses was one of the things he'd missed most about this neighbourhood and he had been the first cat he'd sought out after arriving back.

He lifted his head at the sound of a car door slamming and ran across the lawn. Carlos opened the gate and leaned down to stroke him.

"Hello, Aubrey mate, how you doing?"

Having passed his driving test in the summer, Carlos was now the proud owner of a third-hand Ford which he used to take him to his new job as sous chef in the staff restaurant at the local town hall. While it wasn't the upmarket trendy restaurant that he'd hoped to get his first proper job in, it was, as he'd explained to Aubrey, at least in catering and it would give him some experience of the challenge of mass production of homely food on a limited budget. Swirling dishes through with cream and brandy or picking through fresh green asparagus spears was simply not an option. At the town hall the menu cycled through a weekly repetition and never strayed far from shepherd's pie, fish and chips or a tikka masala plus vegetarian option, with the occasional 'special' when Jamal, the head chef, was feeling creative. But it was fine and he was discovering that he was enjoying it far more than he had thought he would. It also had the undeniable advantage of not involving shifts. The hours were set, the pay was regular, and his colleagues were fun. Jeremy had been pleased, too, pointing out that he would be eligible to contribute to the pension scheme. Carlos had tried not to laugh. He was only just eighteen. Who cared about pensions? That was, like, a million years away. The only cloud on his otherwise sunny horizon was the note.

He had found it this morning. In spite of all staff having personal email, from the chief executive to the cleaners, the council still persisted in the use of old-fashioned wooden pigeonholes placed centrally, and all staff were expected to check them regularly. More often than not they contained nothing other than the odd birthday card or staff pass that had been dropped in the car park, so he had been surprised this morning to see a small white envelope tucked into his. He had pulled out the note and scanned it quickly before stuffing it back into its envelope and making his way towards the kitchens, fighting back the tears that threatened to spill. All morning he had been conscious of its presence festering in his pocket but he had waited until his break to look at it again. The anonymous writer of the note had told him in no uncertain terms that first, he was a bloody foreigner, second, he was taking someone else's job and, third, nobody liked him so why didn't he just get out? He had kept his eyes down while he read it again and again, afraid to look up for fear of seeing a pair of hostile eyes scrutinising him.

He knew about casual racism, of course he did. At school some of the kids had called him Pedro. At first he had been hurt but, although it wasn't all right, he had quickly realised that it didn't really mean anything and that those who employed it just didn't know any better. But the use of those kind of hackneyed nicknames had at least been out in the open. He had never any sense that things were being said behind his back.

This was different. This was sneaky. It was underhand and sly, and there was neither affection nor ignorance behind it. The writer of this note had known exactly the effect it would produce.

He had worked on through the afternoon, checking the pastries and sandwiches for afternoon tea, clearing away and wiping down the work surfaces, talking and smiling to his colleagues as he usually did, but all the time feeling slightly sick. All the time wondering if it was one of them who had written the note, one of them who so bitterly resented his presence in the kitchen. If not one of them, then who? It had to be an employee of the council, that much was clear. It had to have been somebody who had access to the pigeonholes, which wasn't possible without a pass to get into the building. But the council employed hundreds of people, it would be like looking for the proverbial needle in the haystack. And what if, against all the odds, he found out who it was? What would he do about it? Surely it would be better to just ignore it altogether rather than make a big fuss? Whoever had written the note had probably got it off his or her chest now. Maybe they wouldn't do it again. But the nagging thought persisted. What if they did? What if this was just the start? What would he do then?

He had fought against his first inclination, which had been to rip the note up into tiny pieces and flush them down the nearest lavatory, to destroy the loathsome thing for ever. But some instinct had told him that if this was the start of a campaign against him, he would be better off keeping the evidence.

He'd wondered whether to show it to Jamal, but then decided against it. He liked Jamal, he had helped him settle in and he didn't make a fuss when he made a mistake, but if he told him about the note he might feel that he had to do something about it and then there would be all sorts of trouble and he would be at the centre of it. Which would suit whoever it was that hated him in the town hall very well. Anyway, Jamal had been off sick a bit lately and he didn't want to bother him. The best thing, he had decided, was to show it to Jeremy when he got home. Jeremy would know what to do.

He scooped Aubrey up in his arms and felt some of his tension drain away. At least he had Aubrey.

CHAPTER THREE

J eremy watched the girl as she framed her answer. He must stop thinking of her as a girl. She was a grown woman, one of the new members of his staff, and as such likely to be key to his plans for bringing about the change he so earnestly wanted at Sir Franks. He was pleased that she seemed at ease, unlike the previous new teacher that he had scheduled for a little welcome chat that morning. Brett, in his shiny new suit with the trousers straining across his thick thighs and the gold-plated pin clamped across his tie, had seemed slightly fidgety, almost nervous. He had sweated slightly as he stumbled over his responses, as though he thought Jeremy was trying to catch him out. But this girl, sorry, woman, was meeting with him on entirely equal terms. Unlike Brett, she had no difficulty in addressing him as Jeremy. In fact, she hadn't waited to be invited to do so but had simply assumed that they would be on first name terms from the start. How different, he reflected, from his first teaching job. The head at that school, a grammar turned comprehensive, had been distant and remote, almost Victorian in manner, and the thought of ever addressing him by his first name, if he had even known what it was, had never occurred to him.

He had checked her file before the meeting, as he had with all the new teachers, and he had been right about her. She had been educated privately at a girls' school called St Abigails. He had never heard of it, but he had googled it. St Abigail was, apparently, the patron saint of honeybees, beekeepers and ironworkers. Be that as it may, it charged sky high fees and attracted the daughters of the very rich. He had looked at the school website with considerable interest. A large imposing nineteenth-century building, it stood tucked away among lush parklands deep in the west country. With a swimming pool, theatre, and squash courts, it boasted the kind of facilities that schools like Sir Franks barely knew existed, never mind dreamed about.

"And so, Clarissa, what do you think you might find most challenging in your first term with us?" He smiled as he spoke, aware that it was a difficult question to answer honestly but nonetheless one to which he wanted a response. Her answer would at least indicate whether or not she understood anything about the school at which she now worked. She smiled back, a bright confident smile, her perfectly even white teeth bearing testimony to good dentistry.

"Oh, Jeremy. Rissa, please." She paused as she gave the question some thought. Again, unlike the previous young man who had answered immediately, parroting out what he thought would be the expected answer. Namely, that he enjoyed a challenge, without actually specifying what he thought that challenge might be, and that he was always ready to give one hundred and ten per cent, whatever that was supposed to mean. If Jeremy was being cynical he would give Brett two years before he was either stretchered off or on his way to his first promotion at a better school.

He focused again on the young woman before him. He found her beautifully modulated voice strangely restful. He could only hope that it had the same effect on the pupils at Sir Franks.

"I'm well aware, Jeremy, that I have had a number of privileges that many of our pupils here will not have experienced."

He suppressed a grin and resisted the urge to correct her. Precisely none of the pupils at Sir Franks had experienced anything like the start that she had been given in life. Otherwise they wouldn't be at Sir Franks.

"And so," she continued, "I really do feel that I have something to give. That I could bring something to the school, perhaps even help to change some of our pupils lives by showing them that there are other ways to be. By introducing them to possibilities. Although I don't anticipate that being an easy task," she added.

He felt suddenly touched. She was already referring to 'our' pupils. She was obviously sincere. She hadn't needed to take this job as a last resort. She probably hadn't needed to take a job at all. And yet she had chosen to do so. More to the point, she had chosen Sir Franks. He hoped to God that she had a backbone of steel because she was going to need it. With an accent like that she would be a ripe target for the bullies who would take positive pleasure in making her life a misery. At the thought of bullies, his thoughts turned back to the previous evening.

Carlos had been quiet when he returned home from work. Usually buzzing with all that had happened that day, last night he had eaten his dinner with them in almost complete silence. Responding only when spoken to, he had helped to clear the table and then retreated to his room. After several minutes Jeremy had followed him and tapped lightly on his door.

"Is everything all right?"

Carlos, sitting on his bed, had glanced woefully up at him and shaken his head.

"No. Not really."

Jeremy had sat on the small armchair, the only thing that Carlos had brought with him from the flat he had shared with his mother, and regarded him.

"What is it? Do you want to tell me?"

Carlos had fished the note out of his pocket and passed it across. Jeremy had read it and kept his head down, fighting to keep back the rage which had surged through him.

"Where did you get this?"

"At work. It was in my pigeonhole this morning."

Jeremy had felt his anger subside and a lump start to form in his throat. From such an inauspicious start in life, born to an alcoholic father who had deserted his family, and a half-crazy mother, Carlos had arrived in this country as an illegal immigrant. Living in an unlawfully sub-let council flat, the little that he had disintegrated when his mother was murdered. But he had survived. All right, he and Molly had helped by fostering him and giving him a home, but he could so easily have gone off the rails and who would have blamed him? Kids with a far better start in life had ended up behind bars. But Carlos hadn't gone off the rails. He had stayed very firmly on them and had fought against all the odds to become the hard-working decent young man that he was. Never once feeling sorry for himself, he had worked hard at school and catering college and achieved a good set of qualifications. His future was looking bright. Of all the people that deserved a decent break, it had to be Carlos. And now some nasty little bastard had done this to him. Jeremy had cleared his throat before speaking.

"You do know, Carlos, that people who write this kind of thing are generally inadequate?"

Carlos half-smiled. Jeremy always chose the right words. Inadequate was so much better than loser.

"Are they?"

"Trust me. I bet you, whoever wrote this, is some sad sack with no friends. Without a doubt. Someone who writes this kind of garbage does it to make themselves feel important. They have to make other people feel bad before they can feel good. You could almost feel sorry for them."

Almost he had thought, but not quite. People who wrote this kind of thing were dangerous. Hiding behind the cloak of anonymity, with all the stealth of the silent assassin, they had the potential to cause untold damage. Most people had secrets and weaknesses that they would prefer not to have exposed. It was entirely possible that writers of letters such as this one might sometimes hit the mark with disastrous and life-changing consequences.

"And so," he had continued. "We will ignore it. We will chuck it in the bin. Come on. Come downstairs and have a beer with me."

And pushing the note into his pocket he had led the way back downstairs. But he had no intention of chucking the note in the bin. If Carlos received another one he would go to the police. He wasn't certain, but surely sending this kind of message was a criminal offence.

They had spoken no more about it and this morning Carlos had seemed his usual self over breakfast and had gone off to work quite happily. Hopefully he had taken Jeremy's advice and had decided to forget about it.

He drew his mind back to the present as Rissa continued to talk, her eyes alight with enthusiasm.

"And so I thought, Jeremy, that we might have people in to talk to them about career paths. You know, people who are actually doing the job. Like police officers and so on."

Jeremy nodded. It was a good idea, although probably not police officers. Most of the kids at Sir Franks were already well-known to the local constabulary. They didn't need any further introduction. But it was definitely something worth thinking about. When he had first joined the school – years ago when it had been a moderately successful institution – there had been a dedicated part-time careers teacher who had maintained a careers library and held little seminars on the various opportunities available for school leavers. She was long gone now, along with the music teacher and the school nurse. But there was no reason why they couldn't at least attempt something along the lines Rissa was suggesting. And if they planned it properly it would actually cost very little, if anything. It was definitely worth a try and if nothing else, it might help to build links with the local community.

After she had left, leaving a very faint trace of floral perfume behind her, he had sat quietly, thinking. On paper, of all the new staff, she would have seemed the least promising. A posh girl slumming it, who would soon get bored. But in fact, of the five new intakes, she was the one that held out the most hope. He turned to his computer screen and studied her file again. Aged twenty-five, married although she hardly looked old enough, she had given her next of kin as Dean Ingram, who was presumably her husband. Her pre-employment medical questionnaire showed that at one time she had been prone to fainting fits which had been the result of low blood pressure, but the county medical officer had passed her as fit to teach so presumably that wasn't an issue.

Her CV, apart from her academic qualifications, showed that after leaving university she had spent two years doing voluntary teaching and helping to build orphanages overseas. He was impressed. Two years was a long time in a young person's life. She must have been serious about it.

CHAPTER FOUR

A ubrey glanced behind him to check that Moses was keeping up. He smiled as he watched the little black cat staring at a flower, momentarily distracted by an autumn bee alighting on it.

"Come on, Moses."

Moses looked up and scampered forward. Waiting for him to catch up, Aubrey led the way round the side of the house and halted.

"What do you reckon, Vin?"

Vincent looked around, his eyes slightly narrowed as he took in their surroundings.

"Looks okay."

The three cats slipped through the cat flap. It looked, Aubrey thought, different and yet the same. Everything in the kitchen was in the same place but there was a subtle change in the atmosphere. When he had lived here with Molly, Jeremy, and Carlos, it had been somehow friendly and warm. This room seemed a bit cold, almost unlived in. The colours of the walls had changed too. When they had left the house the walls had been painted a pretty shade of light spring green. Now they were a bright white which, with the shiny white tiling, gave the room a faintly unpleasant clinical air. It reminded Aubrey a bit of the vet's consulting room. The table and chairs had gone too which added to the sense of emptiness. Whoever was living here now obviously didn't eat in the kitchen like they used to.

The three cats wandered through to the hall and then stopped. From upstairs came a faint noise and the muted sound of voices. Aubrey turned to Vincent.

"Sounds like somebody's at home."

He felt a sudden feline curiosity to have a look at whoever it was that lived here now. He made a quick calculation. It would be all right. All the downstairs doors were open, he and Vincent could make a quick exit if they were spotted, but there was Moses to consider. Moses wasn't the quickest when it came to the uptake and he couldn't take the risk of him being trapped. He looked down at the little cat who was sitting patiently next to him.

"You wait outside, Moses. We'll be out in a minute."

Aubrey and Vincent watched as Moses trotted obediently back towards the cat flap, and then together they noiselessly crept up the stairs and headed for the room from which the voices were coming. They peered around the door. A man stood with his back to them. He appeared to be getting dressed.

"Can't you stay just a little bit longer? Neil won't be home for hours yet, he's at a meeting in Northampton."

Aubrey and Vincent slipped a little further into the room. In the bed, among the rumpled bedclothes, sheet drawn up to her chin, lay a woman. Aubrey scrutinised her. There was something about her that he didn't like. Tousled straw-coloured hair with a sharp chin and small pale blue eyes set slightly too close together, she looked like the kind of person that a cat should avoid. The man crossed the room and sat down on the bed as he pulled on his socks.

"Sorry, Jeanie, I've got to get back. I've got lots to do and I'm supposed to be at home to let the boiler man in so I really can't stay too long."

"Tell them the boiler man was late."

The man smiled.

"I can't."

The woman stretched out a hand and ran her fingers across his dark hair.

"You work too hard."

The man leaned over and kissed her lightly on the forehead.

"When it suits me." He frowned. "But those patronising posh bastards swanning around the offices with their pathetic little degrees, they wouldn't know a hard day's work if it bit them on their fat arses."

His mouth tightened. It was all right for them. They'd been handed everything on a plate, but he hadn't. Everything he had, he had earned. He'd come a long way from helping his father out at his failing shop. The memory of those early years watching him offer customers two-for-one deals and so-called special offers that would never so much as break even, let alone show a profit, had stuck with him. That, and the fact that his father had seemed to be forever trying to balance the books of the sub-Post Office that somehow always seemed awry no matter how hard he tried, had made him determined to live a different kind of life.

His father had been a kindly, friendly man who, when he was made redundant from the car plant, had relocated the family from the south of England and invested his redundancy money into what had looked from the outside to be a thriving little business. But what had seemed like a golden opportunity to free himself from the nights shifts and be his own boss had turned into a life-sapping gorgon squatting permanently on his shoulders.

The truth was that while his father had been a decent and faithful employee, he had been completely ill-equipped to run any kind of business. He simply didn't have the head for it. No matter how many hours he put in, he couldn't seem to show a decent profit. Under his ownership the shop had drifted into a slow decline. His essentially affable nature had allowed customers to buy food and goods on credit almost indefinitely while his own debts had piled up around him, and as time dragged by he had been at a complete loss to know which way to turn. In the end he'd been drowning in unpaid bills. The small amounts of money that his wife made from various cleaning jobs was nowhere near enough to sustain them. He had died of a heart attack one sunny summer morning, collapsing on the kitchen floor with a faintly surprised smile on his face, leaving his only child alone with his mother in that grim east Anglian town where the wind blew in from the north sea and traditional industries had been allowed to die.

He had been fond of his father but as he had grown older he was determined to be nothing like him. And he wasn't. One of the things he had learned about himself early in life was that he excelled at long-term planning. He was nothing if not patient. When his mother had died he had moved back to the south-east. After a number of false starts and following a temporary contract at the town hall, he had decided that local government was the place for him. It had the great advantage that you didn't need to be from the right background to get in and you couldn't just be made redundant or dismissed at a moment's notice, there were protocols to follow. So he had worked hard, gained professional qualifications, and toadied to all the right people. It had paid off. In the medium term, it suited him. Local government was big enough to offer the opportunities that he wanted but didn't have the cut-throat dynamic of a commercial outfit where the key motivator was money. Not that money didn't attract him, it most certainly did, but he was prepared to take his time on that one. He was even prepared to work for it. Not like that posh lot who thought they were doing the world a favour just by getting out of bed in the morning.

"The way some of them speak to me sometimes," he continued. "You'd think I was sub-human."

The woman reached across and picked up a packet of cigarettes. She shook one free and lit it, inhaling deeply. She smiled, a thin unattractive crinkling of the mouth that brought the latent smokers lines to prominence.

"Just ignore them. You're worth ten of them."

The man took the cigarette from her and drew on it before passing it back. She was right, he was worth ten of them. Twenty. Fifty. But he would bide his time. One day he'd have everything that he wanted, more than any of them had or were ever likely to have. In the meantime he would keep up the façade.

The woman sat up suddenly and screamed, one thin hand clutching the sheet to her chest. A high piercing wail rent the air.

"Oh my God, a stray cat." She pointed a purple painted fingernail towards the door. Oh my God. Do something. I've told Neil time and time again to seal up that bloody cat flap."

CHAPTER FIVE

Aubrey sat tightly curled on Jeremy's lap. It had been a very close thing earlier. Both he and Vincent had been so engrossed in what the man and woman were saying that they had lost some of their usual vigilance and had been taken completely by surprise when the woman had screamed. They had only just made it out in time and had hared off back down the road towards home, pausing only to scoop up Moses who had been waiting patiently outside for them.

Aubrey had been right about the woman though. The way she had reacted, you would have thought that she'd spotted a tiger crouched ready to spring, rather than two ordinary domestic cats who just happened to be in her bedroom. And after all, everybody had to be somewhere. He shivered slightly at the recollection. Something about her shrill reaction had unnerved him.

He looked up as Molly came in.

"Did you finish making the arrangements for the careers fair?"

She passed Jeremy a mug of coffee as she spoke and then settled in her favourite chair. Jeremy nodded.

"Pretty much. You wouldn't believe the paperwork though. And as for the risk assessment..." He laughed suddenly. "If I had honestly assessed the risk of taking Sir Franks pupils for an outing, it would have been the risk to the public, not the kids." He paused. "I just hope to God that we're not making a mistake."

As well he might, thought Aubrey. The last trip that had been organised for pupils at Sir Franks had ended in complete and utter chaos. He had heard Jeremy telling Molly about it after he read the report. Organised three years previously by an art and design teacher that had now, not surprisingly, not only left the school but left teaching, the visit to an art gallery and museum in a neighbouring town had resulted in three arrests, one pupil having his stomach pumped at the local hospital, and an invoice from the coach company for the cleaning and repair of the coach. Since then it had been tacitly understood that there would be no more trips or visits for the foreseeable future.

"Well, it's not far," said Molly. "And you'll be with them."

"True."

Aubrey felt Jeremy sit back and relax slightly.

"It's only on the other side of town and I'll be on the coach with Rissa and two other teachers, and both of them are old hands."

"Why don't you just let them make their own way there? They're old enough and it might be less stressful."

Jeremy gave a rueful smile.

"I did think of that. It would save the cost of the coach apart from anything else. But when I thought it through, I changed my mind. Think about it, Moll. All the work we've been putting in to improving attendance, trusting them to get there under their own steam would be an open invitation to bunk off for the afternoon. It's not a risk worth taking."

He sipped his coffee while he thought about it. Taking some

of their Year Ten pupils to the careers fair, hosted annually for local schools and colleges, had been Rissa's idea. Initially, he'd been sceptical. He knew that the careers fair existed, all the local schools and colleges received advance flyers and emails, but it hadn't really occurred to him to take some of their own pupils, on the basis that they couldn't be trusted to behave themselves. But Rissa had been keen to stress that it would be a first step in showing them that there was what she called 'another way'. It would also, she had pointed out with a practicality that had surprised him, be easy to round them up if they misbehaved or tried to escape. The fair was being held in the town hall. The teaching staff could take it in turns to patrol the doors.

He thought about Rissa for a moment. She was proving to be surprisingly popular with the pupils. He had feared that her posh accent combined with her eagerness to help turn the school around would be like a red rag to some of their more feral pupils. But against all the odds she had not only survived but positively prospered. There was something about her that seemed to command attention, both in and out of the classroom. Probably all that private school educating, he thought. It gave an inner confidence, an air of quiet self-assurance that was difficult to acquire in later life. She assumed that she was in charge in the classroom and that the pupils would do as she told them, and by and large most of them did.

In line with his policy of observing all his staff teach at least once a year, he had visited her classroom yesterday. All right, she hadn't quite worked miracles. A couple of the layabouts at the back were resting their heads on their desks, enveloped in their usual stupor of disengagement, but at least they weren't fighting or listening to music. Most of the rest of the class appeared to be reasonably well focused and one or two even put their hands up to answer questions. He had stayed longer than he had proposed and had left the classroom feeling a renewed sense of optimism in the future of Sir Franks.

CHAPTER SIX

Jeremy glanced down at his watch and breathed a sigh of relief. It was nearly time to go home and so far there had been no incidents. All the kids had turned up as required and there had been no fights on the coach. Neither had there been, so far, any attempts at escape. In fact, they actually appeared to be enjoying themselves. Quite a number of them had willingly picked up the leaflets and information sheets that they had been offered, as well as all the free pens, notebooks, Post-it notes and other stationery items that each stall had given them. He had been half amused and half saddened by the sight of them quickly stuffing all their freebies in the canvas tote bags that they had been furnished with on arrival, as if they were afraid they'd be snatched away again. In any event he had to admit, in spite of his earlier misgivings, the trip had been a success.

He looked around him. He had always thought the town hall a rather forbidding building, a remnant of late Victorian civic pride and wealth with all its dark panelling and polished bannisters. The huge, almost baronial fireplaces hadn't been lit since the middle of the last century, but they were swept and cleaned along with everything else as a matter of course. The town hall was where part of his interview for the Sir Franks headship had been held. That had been in a big, gloomy room dominated by portraits of long dead local dignitaries and a large highly-polished mahogany table. It hadn't exactly been conducive to relaxation, but then he supposed that it wasn't meant to be. It was a room intended for serious business. But the room that they were using for the careers fair was in the modern extension at the back. It was large, bright, and airy, normally used for public meetings, with big windows and plenty of space to move around in, a testament to the more free-spirited twenty-first century architecture.

He checked his watch again. He just had time to visit the cloakroom before they started rounding the kids up ready to go home and he could take this damned name badge off. He'd always hated wearing ID but all teaching staff had been issued with one on arrival which bore their name and the name of their school, and it had been made clear that they were expected to wear them, presumably so that they could be quickly identified if any of the kids caused a nuisance.

Slipping out through the door he made his way down the corridor and then stopped as he heard a slight snuffling sound. It sounded as though it was coming from what looked like a cupboard. Curious, he moved towards it and listened harder. There it was again, louder this time and accompanied by a small wailing sound. He jumped back as the cupboard door suddenly opened to reveal a girl standing among a clutter of mops and buckets. She looked up startled, the traces of tears clearly marked on her face. Jeremy stared at her for a moment. She was small and pretty with clear blue-grey eyes, honey-coloured hair and a heart-shaped face. She looked very familiar.

"Mr Goodman. Hello, sir."

The girl stepped out and sniffed as she spoke, one hand

clutching a damp, crumpled tissue. Jeremy took a step back. Of course, it was Chloe Kennedy. He'd taught her a few years ago, just before he had left Sir Franks to become an inspector. Nice girl, a little shy, but capable enough when encouraged. She had, if he recalled correctly, been the eldest of six siblings who were all a product of what was euphemistically called a troubled family. As a result she and her brothers and sisters had spent a large part of their childhood in and out of care. So what was she doing in a cupboard at the town hall?

"I don't expect you remember me, sir."

"Of course I do." Jeremy spoke warmly. "It's Chloe, isn't it?" He paused. "Are you all right?"

He realised as soon as he spoke that it was a foolish question. Of course she wasn't all right, otherwise she wouldn't be crying in a cupboard.

Chloe pulled another tissue from her pocket, blew her nose, and nodded. She gave a faint watery smile.

"I work here, sir," she said, looking around her. There was an unmistakeable note of pride in her voice. "In the housing department. After I left school, I retook my GCSEs at college."

And, thought Jeremy, had obviously passed them with sufficiently good grades to get a job at the town hall. He felt a sudden rush of pride, tinged with sadness. Pride that Chloe had decided to improve her lot. Sad that she had needed to do it in the first place. Sir Franks had let her down. Although, he recalled, suddenly feeling more cheered, she had passed her GCSE English, which had been in his class.

"That's excellent, Chloe. You've done really well."

And he meant it. She had done very well indeed. Starting a career with a local authority was no mean feat, especially for a former pupil of Sir Frank Wainwright's, a depressingly large number of whom seemed to end up in dead-end jobs with no prospects whatsoever. That is, if they ended up with a job at all.

So why had Chloe been crying? He studied her more closely. Perhaps she'd broken up with a boyfriend or something. If so, it was no good him telling her that it wasn't the end of the world, that she'd get over it, that in six months' time it would all look completely different and that she'd probably have met someone else by then. She wouldn't believe it any more than he would have done at her age. He looked down at his watch. It felt wrong to just leave her here but the coach was due in five minutes. And if it was boyfriend trouble there was nothing much he could do about it anyway.

"It's the letters, sir." Chloe suddenly burst into tears again. "I keep getting them."

He made a quick decision.

"Chloe, what time do you finish work?"

CHAPTER SEVEN

Jeremy stirred his coffee slowly, watching the girl sitting opposite him as she cupped her small hands around the mug of hot chocolate that he had bought her. He liked this café. It had been here for years. Situated opposite the town hall, it was bright, cheerful and reasonably priced. It was one of the few surviving independents and somehow or other it seemed to have limped through every recession, every economic downturn, and still make the best coffee in town. The owner, Alfonso, was nice too, a large jolly man who was a permanent fixture on Aubrey and Vincent's local rounds. Unknown to Jeremy, they usually dropped by just after closing. Partly to visit Alfonso's cat, Muriel, who had recently ended up on the losing side in an altercation with a motorbike and was confined to quarters for the time being, but also to hoover up any leftovers Alfonso put out for them.

Overall, Jeremy thought that it had been a good idea to meet Chloe here. It was public and central, so nobody could accuse him of anything untoward. Although, he reflected, it was a sorry state of affairs when a young person's former teacher couldn't lend a listening ear without fear of being denounced as some sort of pervert. Chloe put her mug down and looked back at him. A faint smear of chocolate smudged against the side of her mouth. She looked suddenly very young.

"The thing is, sir..."

Jeremy put his hand up, palm outwards.

"Mr Goodman, please."

He couldn't ask her to call him Jeremy. It would, he knew, be a step too far and might inhibit her from talking altogether. When he and Molly occasionally encountered former pupils in the town when they were out shopping, they still often addressed him as sir, even though they were now in their thirties. He was used to it, although it always took Molly by surprise. Chloe smiled, a faint dimpling that relieved some of the stress on her face.

"Mr Goodman. The thing is, it's the letters."

Years of teaching had taught him that conversation with teenagers wasn't always linear. In fact, talking to the average sixteen-year-old was a bit like the caucus race in Alice, where the Dodo just yelled go and all the animals ran around until the Dodo declared that the race was over and that they'd all won. It was fine, he was used to it. He'd just pick up where Chloe had started and take it from there. He could fill in any gaps later, although he had a nasty suspicion that he knew what was coming.

"What about them?"

Chloe reached down and hauled her handbag up from the floor. He watched as she rummaged around in it and pulled out several pieces of creased paper.

"It's these, sir... Mr Goodman."

He took the sheets that she passed him and smoothed them out on the table. They were written on the same kind of paper that the note to Carlos had been, a standard ordinary sheet of white printing paper. The kind used in homes and offices all over the country. He was fairly sure that they had been written by the same person that had written the note to Carlos. Apart from what appeared to him to be similar styles, the likelihood of two poison pen writers operating in the same building at the same time was remote to say the least. He began reading.

In the first note Chloe was, the writer asserted, no better than she ought to be. He smiled grimly. That was an old-fashioned expression, if ever he'd heard one. It was one of the things that his grandmother used to say and, as a boy, it had always confused him. If you were only as good as you ought to be, then wasn't that good enough? Pushing reminiscences of the grim old lady away, he read on.

Using a smattering of good old-fashioned Anglo-Saxon words, the writer informed Chloe that she was just like her mother, a no good drunken whore who sold her favours all over town. Not only that, but her father was a drug-raddled thief who spent most of his time in and out of prison. The second note went on to inform Chloe that the council didn't want people like her dragging them down, that she shouldn't be allowed to mix with respectable people, and that she ought to get back to the gutter where she belonged. The third note repeated much of what was contained in the first note with the added embellishment of detailing the kind of diseases that parents like hers carried.

He looked up at his former pupil.

"Chloe," he began, and then stopped. It would probably be better to let her speak freely rather than prompt her. She looked at him and then down at the letters.

"They started coming about two weeks ago. I didn't know what to do." She swallowed hard and took a deep breath. "The thing is, Mr Goodman, my mum and dad, they, well, they..." she tailed off and bit her bottom lip.

Jeremy remembered her parents, at least he remembered

her mother. It would be difficult to forget her. He didn't think he'd ever had the dubious pleasure of meeting the father although he'd heard about him. A byword in the town, he was a living stereotype of benefit cheating, drug-taking, feckless idleness. He was the kind of person who caused trouble wherever he went, who had been barred from the majority of pubs in the area, and was frequently seen sporting an electronic tag. The last Jeremy had heard, he was back in prison. But he had met the mother. She had come to a parents' evening once. A big, blowsy lump of a woman with a low-cut top and heavily made-up face, she had sat down and breathed gin fumes all over him. While he had been speaking, she had just stared at him silently, her expression completely blank, to the point where he had wondered if anything that he was saying was actually going in. When he had finished she had simply got up and left. But she had at least turned up, even if it was only the once, so presumably she cared something for Chloe. Some of the parents of the pupils at Sir Franks never came to parents' evenings at all. As far as they were concerned, school and everything it represented, was the enemy and not to be engaged with at any price.

He regarded Chloe now. In some ways she reminded him of Carlos. She had the same look of hopeful innocence, tempered by bitter experience.

"What the letters said about my parents, well..." Chloe paused and then continued, her words tumbling out now in a rush. "They can't help it, Mr Goodman. They do try. It's just that..." she tailed off again.

Just what, he wondered. Just that they always put themselves first, like all addicts did? Somebody had once told him that the one thing that addicts wanted was more. And he guessed that was about right. The fact that they were responsible for six children between them appeared largely irrelevant compared to their own needs. People like Chloe's parents were more interested in where their next drink or fix was coming from than putting a half decent meal on the table or making sure their children went to bed at a reasonable time so they'd be awake for school the next morning.

As if reading his mind, Chloe spoke again.

"We always had something to eat and everything. There was always beans and cocoa pops and stuff. And when they had some money we sometimes used to get pizzas."

He stared at her. Good God. That was setting the bar pretty low.

"And we did have a washing machine," she continued. "So I could do all our school blouses and shirts and everything on a Sunday."

While her parents were at the pub, presumably. Chloe had done a good job by her brothers and sisters, he thought. If he recalled correctly, the Kennedy children's clothes were always clean, if not ironed. He gave an inward sigh. As teachers they often had absolutely no idea about their pupils home lives. It was all very well giving some kid a bollocking for not wearing the right uniform, but if they didn't have it they couldn't wear it. Which was something else to add to his ever-growing list of concerns to address. He gathered up the letters in front of him.

"Have you told anybody else about these?"

"I did tell the department manager when I got the second one. I wasn't sure whether to, but then I thought I ought to show him, so I did."

"And what did he say?"

"He said to just ignore it. He said it was probably somebody playing a joke or something."

Hardly, thought Jeremy. The point of a joke is that it's supposed to be funny. And telling Chloe to ignore it wasn't the best advice to give a frightened and unhappy young girl. He was probably overworked and underpaid and didn't want to get involved, but he could have at least pretended to take it seriously.

He looked at Chloe's trusting face.

"Do you want me to take these away?"

Chloe nodded. She stared down at the table for a moment before speaking.

"I don't want people at work to know about my mum and dad."

Much chance of keeping that secret, thought Jeremy. He doubted there was anyone in the town who didn't know them, at least by sight, but he could hardly tell her that. Whatever her parents were like, their sins were not hers. She shouldn't have to be going through this.

Like Carlos, in spite of the odds and the decidedly weighted hand she had been dealt, she was showing every sign of making something of her life, and now someone was bent on spoiling it for her. He choked down the rage that suddenly threatened to engulf him and took a deep breath. Showing anger wasn't going to help Chloe. She was upset enough as it was. When he spoke he kept his tone deliberately calm.

"You know, Chloe, the writer of these letters is almost certainly a sick person. This isn't about you, it's about them." He paused. He wasn't sure where he was going with this. He wanted to say something comforting, something to reassure her, but what? It was all very well telling her that the poison pen was sick and twisted, that what he or she had written was just nonsense to be disregarded. Even if Chloe believed him, that wouldn't draw the venom or make the letters stop. He wondered suddenly if Chloe and Carlos had been the only recipients.

"Chloe, I don't suppose you know if anybody else has received these letters?"

"I'm not sure, Mr Goodman. But I did see Miss Bates

coming out of the disabled toilet the other day and she looked like she'd been crying. She uses a wheelchair," she added.

Jeremy nodded, his expression thoughtful. Miss Bates could have been crying for any number of reasons. Perhaps she'd just been having a bad day. God knew, he felt like weeping himself often enough after a particularly trying time at school. But he doubted that the town hall posed the same kind of challenges as Sir Franks. What he suspected to be far more likely was that Miss Bates had been crying because of something particularly nasty that somebody had written to her. Somebody anonymous, somebody who claimed the freedom to walk in and out of people's lives spreading unhappiness and despair. Somebody who clearly felt that they could act with impunity, and that of course was part of the problem. The recipients of these repugnant letters had no right of reply. The writer could keep shooting round corners as long as he liked. Or as long as he wasn't stopped. He reached for a paper napkin and scribbled on it.

"Chloe, take this. It's my mobile number. Text or call me if you receive any more letters."

Chloe took the napkin and, folding it carefully, stowed it in her handbag.

"What are you going to do, Mr Goodman?"

Good question. What *was* he going to do? At least he could lift some of the burden from Chloe's shoulders. He smiled reassuringly.

"I'm not sure yet. But leave it with me."

CHAPTER EIGHT

J eremy had driven past it many times but it had never really registered in his consciousness, so he hadn't ever recognised it for what it was. Situated on the road leading out of town, set back among what looked like a small industrial estate, was a low, grey unedifying building with a narrow entrance and darkened windows, so that presumably whoever was inside could see out, but passers-by couldn't see in. The architect who had designed it hadn't had the words welcoming or friendly in their brief, that was for sure. So much for building community relations, this place looked about as welcoming as a mortuary on a wet Sunday afternoon.

He parked the car in the small visitors car park and looked up. There didn't appear to be any lights on, but with those windows, it was difficult to tell. Surely there was somebody in there. All right, it was after six in the evening, but criminals didn't keep office hours, and neither did police officers. Or did they? He realised suddenly that he didn't have a clue. For all he knew, they clocked off at five and locked the door behind them. He'd had very little contact with the local police, it being mostly confined to when they turned up at Sir Franks seeking information about a suspected miscreant.

He thought back to the police station in the town where he'd been brought up. It couldn't have been more different to this one. He'd somehow thought, he supposed, that police stations were pretty much the same everywhere. He couldn't have been more wrong. The police station of his childhood had been near the centre of town, a warm, red-brick building that still had the iconic blue lamp outside. Everybody knew where it was and, while the door hadn't always been literally open, it had been metaphorically open so that anybody could walk in. Jeremy had gone in there once when he was about ten and his bicycle had been stolen. He had left it outside the library and when he came out it had gone. He had been greeted with grave respect by the desk sergeant who had noted down all the details – including the stickers with which he had lovingly adorned the crossbar – and promised that they would look for it.

And look for it they had. It had been found by the railway station, presumably borrowed by somebody who couldn't be bothered to walk the half mile from the town centre. Would he, he wondered, as a ten-year-old boy, have been quite so comfortable approaching this building? Somehow he doubted it.

Climbing out of the car he walked towards the entrance and pressed the intercom.

"Yes?"

The voice was gruff, but not unfriendly.

Jeremy cleared his throat.

"I've come to report a crime. I think," he added, as the electronic door slid open.

Inside, the room was lit by a single fluorescent tube that threw a cold light on the little group of hard-back chairs that stood in a regimented line and presumably constituted a waiting area. From another room he could hear the low thrum of voices.

So there were officers in the building, they hadn't all gone home for the evening. He walked towards the desk. A tired looking middle-aged man stood behind it. He glanced up at the clock on the wall and then back towards Jeremy.

"So, sir. This crime that you think you might have come to report?"

Jeremy pulled Chloe's letters out and spread them in front of him.

"It's these. They were sent to a young person that I know, and there's been another one sent to somebody else."

He turned and looked about him while the officer slowly read the letters. Blu-Tacked notices on the walls reminded him to mark his valuable possessions and to observe the speed limits, while a vending machine in the corner had an out of order sign slung across it. High up above the entrance a tattered piece of tinsel hung limply down, a remnant from some Christmas party, he guessed. A framed certificate informed visitors that the constabulary were Investors In People. But not, presumably, in interior design. God, this place was as depressing on the inside as it was on the outside. It made Sir Franks look like a positive tourism hotspot. He turned back as the officer spoke.

"Can I ask how you came to be in possession of the letters, sir?"

"They were sent to my foster son and to a former pupil of mine. They showed them to me."

The officer rubbed his hand across his chin.

"One for Rench, I think."

"Rench?"

Jeremy frowned. Was that a euphemism for the bin?

"Rench," the officer repeated. "DC Renshaw. This sort of thing is right up his street. He's done all the courses. As it happens he's on duty this evening. Do you want to come through, sir?"

Jeremy followed the officer through a side door and into a small inner room. This area was much less depressing than the outer room. It was warm for a start, and was furnished with several easy chairs and a polished coffee table. Presumably it was reserved for those deemed to be respectable visitors. Leaving Jeremy on his own, the officer left and returned several minutes later, accompanied by a smart young man with thick blond hair, a wide smile, and a rather well-cut suit. Jeremy smiled to himself. Here was a poster boy for fast-track promotion if ever he'd seen one. He'd put money on it that he was fresh out of university. The young man laid an iPad on the table and held out his hand.

"Good evening, sir. My name is Detective Constable Renshaw. I understand that you've received some unpleasant letters?"

"Not me personally," said Jeremy. "Two young people that I know. I suspect that some other people might have received some too. The thing is, I'm not sure if it's a crime or not."

DC Renshaw gestured to him to sit down and took the chair opposite.

"It certainly is a crime."

Flicking open the iPad, he quickly ran his fingers over the screen and turned it to show Jeremy.

"As you can see, sir. It's classed as malicious communication."

Jeremy was intrigued. Malicious wasn't a word that you encountered much these days. In fact he couldn't remember the last time he'd heard it, but it had a rather wonderfully sinister ring to it.

"Basically it means sending somebody a letter or note, or, these days, posting online, something with the intention to cause distress or anxiety. It's usually done anonymously," DC Renshaw continued. "I don't think there's much doubt that the writer of your letters intended to cause distress or anxiety."

Jeremy peered down at the screen again and then looked up at DC Renshaw.

"And do people get prosecuted for it?" he asked.

The officer nodded.

"A few do. To some extent it depends on the circumstances. If it's someone sitting at home alone with too much time on their hands and not enough to do, we generally find that a firm word sorts it out. Those cases are usually pretty mild, accusations against neighbours and so on. Once they know that we're onto them it tends to stop. Others are a bit more complex. There was a case in the Midlands last year where a young man was receiving some really nasty stuff. Explicit, if you know what I mean."

Unfortunately, thought Jeremy, he rather thought that he did know.

"And did they find out who did it?" he asked.

"Oh yes. She got six months."

"She?"

"The joke was that she was a magistrate. He'd been in court when she was on the bench. That was how she'd got all the background info on him, including his address and where he worked. It seems that she had developed some sort of obsession with him. The suspicion was that she'd sent other young men letters too, but they didn't come forward."

"I suppose some people are reluctant to report it?"

Even as he spoke, Jeremy realised the truth of what he was saying. Fear of publicly exposing her parents for what they were had made Chloe complicit in the nastiness of the business, and he doubted that Carlos would be willingly showing the note that he'd received to any of his friends.

"Well, sir, you can see why. I guess it's understandable that people would be embarrassed. But as an offence, it's becoming more popular." He paused and frowned slightly, conscious that he'd chosen the wrong word. "What I mean is, more people are doing it. Because of all the online possibilities. For some reason they think it makes them more safe if they do it from behind a screen."

Jeremy thought about it. It was true. Some people wrote some pretty unpleasant things on social media, to the point where he thought it rightly ought to be called anti-social media. He'd only recently come to social media himself, but he was already aware of the spiteful and sometimes outright defamatory material that was posted. Being gratuitously unpleasant seemed to give a platform to some people who couldn't validate themselves in any other way. But DC Renshaw was right, it was the anonymity of the keyboard that enabled it. That screen was an effective hiding place. And it wasn't just adults who engaged in it. He'd read about children in neighbouring counties being bullied online, on a couple of occasions with tragic consequences. Of course there had always been bullying, it wasn't a new problem, but this was different. This didn't stop when the school bell rang. This followed kids home and into their bedrooms. The internet didn't recognise closed doors.

"How do you catch these people if they're doing it online?" he asked.

DC Renshaw smiled.

"Once they're online it actually makes it easier for us to trace them, because in the right circumstances we can often track the IP address. It was much harder in the old days when letters were just put in a post box. And tracking a mobile is a piece of cake these days, too."

Jeremy sighed.

"I guess then, on that basis, these," he pointed towards the letters that DC Renshaw had fanned out on the table, "are going to be difficult to trace. Although," he added, "they were sent within an organisation and placed in an area where only employees have access."

The officer's face brightened.

"Really, sir? That's very helpful. So where is that exactly?"

"The town hall," said Jeremy.

DC Renshaw's face fell again.

"Ah. Well, leave it with me, sir. I'll see what we can come up with. If you let me have your mobile number, I'll keep you updated if we uncover anything."

He fished in his pocket for a small card and handed it to Jeremy. "In the meantime, let us know if your youngsters receive any more of them."

CHAPTER NINE

The man listened irritably as the printer made that horrible grinding sound while it ripped up another sheet of paper. He really did need to replace it, he'd had it for years and it was a cheap number to start with. He strode over to it and yanked open the cover, leaning forward to tease out the crumpled sheet caught between the rollers. He dropped it in the wastepaper bin and, turning back to his computer, pressed print again. He really needed it to work this evening.

Five seconds later he pulled on his thin latex gloves and caught the fresh sheet as it rolled out. He breathed a sigh of satisfaction. This one was an absolute gift, completely irresistible. It was pure luck that he'd seen them this evening. He'd only popped out to get some wine but the supermarket car park had been unusually full, so he'd parked up at the back under the trees. And there they'd been, mouths clamped together and hands rambling all over the place. Mr Goody Two Shoes Harker, married HR manager and all-time pain in the arse, and Ms Dombey, his uptight, hatchet-faced assistant. Folding the sheet neatly in two he slipped it into a small freezer bag and then pulled his gloves off.

All in all it had been a good day, what with this and Jeannie texting him this morning to say that her old man was away for the day. After he'd rung in to work to say that he'd be late because he had to wait in for the boiler man, he'd driven straight over there. She was a good sort, was Jeannie. He didn't think that he loved her, but then he wasn't sure that he understood what love was anyway. They were kindred spirits, two of a kind, and that was the important thing. Slightly older than him, she was out for what she could get out of life and so was he. If everything worked out then they had a real future together.

He turned back to his computer and clicked open the file marked correspondence. He read the message he'd left a couple of days ago again. It was the first one that he'd done outside of work and it was, he had to admit, rather a good one. He'd recently discovered an online thesaurus, after which his creative juices had really started to flow. He wished that he could have been there to see him open it. He bet it had wiped that irritating smile off his fat face. He smiled to himself. There was no doubt that it felt good, positively masterful, to have such power. And these people, they deserved it. It wasn't like they didn't have it coming to them.

That boy Carlos, for instance. He was far too cocky, much too sure of himself. He'd seen the way some of the women looked at him. He needed taking down a peg or two. He should keep his head down like he had at his age and not go around looking so bloody cheerful all the time. And that Miss Bates with her stupid saintly expression, he was sick of the sight of her. She'd wasted hundreds of pounds of the council's money on all those so-called reasonable adjustments, none of which were necessary in his opinion. If she couldn't do her job, tough shit. She shouldn't have been given it in the first place. As for that Chloe Kennedy and her disgusting family, people like that shouldn't be allowed within a million miles of decent people like him. When he thought of them, words almost failed him. Almost, but not quite.

He leaned back in his chair and clasped his hands behind his head. He felt pleasantly contented. From downstairs, he could hear the familiar opening music of the stupid costume drama that his wife always watched. He couldn't stand it himself. He preferred crime any day, and preferably true crime. He liked the historic ones best, those from the Victorian and Edwardian era. There was a kind of gothic drama about them that appealed to him. Some of the twenties and thirties ones were good, too. He was less keen on the modern cases though. They were too coarse, too in your face. There was just not enough finesse about them in his opinion. But the old cases, they were the real deal. Crippen, George Joseph Smith, John Haigh, Mary Ann Cotton, Christie, they were masters of the art.

He'd first discovered them when he was a teenager and he'd been captivated from the start. He should, he often thought, have been a criminologist. He would have been brilliant at it. If he'd had the opportunity he could have studied it properly and written books about it, instead of just reading other peoples'. He could have lectured on it, and presented television programmes, too. He would have been a lot better than those amateurs that currently appeared on the screen with their posh voices and stupid mannerisms. Given the chance, he could have had a whole different life. But he hadn't been given the chance. He hadn't been given anything but his father's debts and an ailing mother.

His mind ran back again to his parents. They were in his thoughts a lot lately, although he wasn't sure why. Perhaps because his life now was such a contrast to theirs. Aged well before their time, they had done nothing but struggle all their days. They had taken only one holiday that he could remember, and that had been a week at the seaside when he was about four.

They never ate out and they never visited the cinema, let alone a theatre. His father's death, although sudden and premature, had been, he thought, timely. He had been a proud man, but given the shambles that he had made of the business, what did he have to look forward to but bankruptcy and all the shame that he would have felt along with it? That sudden and dramatic collapse on the kitchen floor had released him.

His mother hadn't escaped quite so mercifully. Heartbroken and confused following her husband's death, she had descended into a gentle chaos in which she appeared unable to make sense of the world around her. As her only surviving relative, it had been made clear to him by the authorities that it was down to him to ensure her welfare. It had been a grim existence and one which he had been only too pleased to escape from.

He sat forward again and rested his elbows down on the cheap laminate unit that he used as a desk. One day he'd have a proper desk. An oak one with a roll top and lots of drawers, like the sort that posh solicitors had in the old movies, and he'd have a big house to put it in with a double garage outside where he'd keep his new Mercedes. He would take Jeannie there to live with him. Everything that he wanted would be his, because he deserved it. He sat back and closed his eyes.

CHAPTER TEN

A ubrey strolled round the side of the café and slipped through the cat flap into the small living quarters at the back. He was looking forward to seeing Muriel. Among the cat world, Muriel was considered to be something of an intellectual. He didn't think that she could actually read, but she always knew what words meant and stuff like that, and she was very wise. If any of them were bothered by something that they'd seen or overheard, they usually went to Muriel for advice.

Lying on her bed, Muriel raised a paw in greeting.

"All right, Aubrey? How's it going?"

"Not too bad, Muriel. Not too bad."

"Where's Vincent?"

"He'll be along later. He's taken Moses down to the canal for a spot of fishing."

Climbing out of her basket, Muriel limped across the room and joined Aubrey.

"How's the leg now?" he asked.

"Getting there," said Muriel.

"Alfonso about?"

"In the café."

Together they walked through the small side door into the café and watched as Alfonso flipped the open sign to closed and pulled down the blind. He looked, thought Aubrey, not quite his usual ebullient self. He looked in fact as though he was worried about something. He turned to Muriel.

"What's up with him?"

Muriel shrugged.

"I don't know. He's off his food though."

Aubrey was shocked. Being off your food was a serious business, especially for someone like Alfonso who enjoyed eating almost more than any human he knew. In fact, in that respect, he could have been a cat.

They watched as Alfonso suddenly sat down at one of the little checked table-clothed tables and dropped his head into his hands. Alarmed, Aubrey ran across the room and laid a paw on his knee. Alfonso looked up and gave a small half-smile. Reaching down he ran a hand over Aubrey's head and then hauled him onto his lap. Staring into Aubrey's green-gold eyes, he spoke slowly.

"Tell me, cat, what is it that I am going to do? I really do not know. Last week, all was well. I was happy. I would wake in the morning and look forward to the day. Now everything has changed. This week, I open my eyes and I dread what the day will bring..." He paused and swallowed before continuing. "Never before have such things been said to me. Never."

Aubrey sat quietly while Alfonso looked away and stared at the wall, his expression bleak. When he spoke again his voice was quiet, almost a whisper.

"This café, this business, it is all I have. I have been here for many years. My customers, they are my friends, more than friends. They are like family to me."

Alfonso had once had a wife Aubrey knew, because Muriel had told him, but she had died a long time ago. There was no other family other than a niece, his late brother's daughter, but she rarely visited. In fact Muriel said that she had only seen her three or four times and she had lived with Alfonso for nearly ten years.

"And it is lies. All of it. Wicked lies. But what can I say? Some people, they will think that it is true. Because there is no smoke without fire. That is what they will think. No smoke without fire," he repeated.

Alfonso looked down at Aubrey again, his face sombre.

"And I go to the park to walk. Why else should I go there? It is what it is made for. It is what people do. It is a nice place."

Aubrey agreed. The park was a very nice place, he and Vincent often went over there to lark about when the weather was nice and when it wasn't nice they could sit in one of the shelters and watch the world go by. They'd had a go on the slide once, but Aubrey hadn't really liked it. Too quick, not enough control. Quite nice to just sit at the top though, you could see for miles around. The swings were all right. You could just jump up and sort of sway about a bit.

"Of course," continued Alfonso, "I go there in the evenings because I am here all day. When other time can I go for a walk? I have no garden, only the courtyard, and there is no pleasure to simply walk around the streets. The park, it is a nice place," he repeated. "And why should I not go there?"

Alfonso suddenly thumped his fist down on the table, making Aubrey jump.

"It is not true. There is no truth. I do not watch people. I do not go spying on courting couples. I do not hide in bushes so that I can open my trousers and jump out and frighten people. That is something that only the perverts do. The sick twisted people. And I am not a pervert!" Alfonso raised his voice and thumped his fist down again. "I go to the park to walk, to look at the flowers, to get the fresh air!"

Aubrey glanced over at Muriel. She looked back, her face worried. Reaching into his apron pocket, Alfonso pulled out a small white envelope and shook out the sheet of paper within. He stared down at it and spoke again, his expression sad and his voice quieter this time.

"And now I must look at all my customers again, because it must be one of them who left it here, in the toilet." He smiled suddenly. "Which is the right place for it."

The smile dropped from his face and he looked serious again.

"But now I must watch all my customers, because one of them left it there. One of them is not my friend."

CHAPTER ELEVEN

The noise from the classroom was reaching a crescendo. From a room at the end of the corridor, where Jeremy was emerging from a meeting, it hit him with force. He hurried towards it. Whatever was going on in there wasn't good. He flung open the classroom door and marched in. On the floor space which had been created by pushing the desks back, two boys were going at it hammer and tongs. Surrounding them, the rest of the class shouted encouragement while atop a desk, feet astride and notebook in hand, one of the girls was calling the odds.

He rushed in and raised his voice.

"What on earth is going on in here?" Which was, he had to admit, a stupid question. It was perfectly clear what was going on. "Where's your teacher?"

The two boys reluctantly pulled away from each other as the rest of the class fell silent. While many of the pupils at Sir Franks viewed the teaching staff as more or less irrelevant, being the head teacher still carried some weight.

"She's not here, sir," said one of the boys.

Jeremy resisted the urge to tell the boy not to state the

bleeding obvious. Even the weakest teachers at Sir Franks didn't have full-scale fights going on under their noses.

"Who's meant to be in here with you?"

The girl standing on the desk climbed reluctantly down.

"Mrs Ingram. Sir," she added.

Jeremy felt a stab of bitter disappointment. Rissa. Had she got fed up with Sir Franks already? She hadn't rung or emailed in sick, he knew. Every morning, his secretary, or chief administrator to give her her correct title, gave him a list of absentee staff and he'd been pleased to note of late that there had been fewer ringing or emailing with the obligatory hacking cough or vague descriptions of 'having eaten something'.

His current top of the absentee pops were the probationers, as he still thought of them. He wasn't surprised. New teachers, faced with hundreds of fresh germs every day, often took a while to build up the necessary resilience. But Rissa hadn't been among them. She hadn't had a single day off since the start of term. He'd give her a call later and find out what was going on.

In the meantime, he had to sort this lot out. He'd step in and teach the class himself, but he had so much to do this morning that he simply couldn't spare the time. Some poor sod was about to give up their free period.

———

Jeremy locked his car and strolled up the front path, eyes down and his expression thoughtful. Rissa's mobile had gone straight to answerphone each time he had rung and he wasn't quite sure what to do next. Her knew her address, it was on file, but somehow it didn't seem right to just turn up at her house. It felt almost like bullying and although he could be accused of a number of failings, being a bully wasn't one of them. But what if something was seriously wrong? He supposed he could ask one of the female members of staff, or perhaps his secretary, to call round if she didn't make contact by tomorrow. He felt suddenly irritated.

If she was ill or there had been some sort of family crisis she should have rung in so they could cover her classes, not just abandoned ship and dropped off the radar. Or, if for whatever reason, she didn't feel like talking, she could at least have emailed or asked her husband to ring on her behalf. He looked up and smiled as Molly called out from the open front room window.

"Carlos is making a barbecue in the back garden. It's nearly ready."

He walked round the side of the house and lifted his nose to the smoky charcoal fumes drifting towards him. It was such an enticing smell. It reminded him of holidays and sunshine and made him want to eat, even if he wasn't hungry. He felt his earlier irritation lift. A barbecue was just what he needed to cheer him up. Sod the diet. He'd start again tomorrow.

On the patio area Carlos stood, tongs at the ready and his expression grave, as he stared down at the grill. By his feet Aubrey and Vincent sat patiently, more in hope than expectation. Jeremy threw his briefcase to the ground, loosened his tie, and pulled back one of the garden chairs.

"This all looks very jolly."

He resisted the urge to rub his hands together in a sign of appreciation. It was exactly the sort of gesture that both his father and his grandfather used to make and, of late, he had been growing increasingly aware that he was becoming exactly like them. Not that they were bad men, far from it, but he wasn't ready to cede his individuality just yet. Molly placed a large jug on the table, the big chunks of ice clinking together as she set it down.

"Mojito. I thought it would make a nice change for such a

lovely evening. The barbecue was Carlos's idea. It might be our last opportunity before autumn sets in properly."

Jeremy poured them all a drink from the jug and gave a sigh of satisfaction. He was home and all was right with the world. He'd forget about Rissa until tomorrow. And if it turned out that his first suspicion of her was correct, that she was a posh girl slumming it, who would soon get bored, well, so be it. It wasn't the end of the world. Worse things happened at sea, as his father used to say. He turned to Molly.

"So how was your day?"

He was conscious that, since starting the headship at Sir Franks, he had been so preoccupied that he hadn't paid much attention to Molly's voluntary work. All right, he knew that she was only volunteering while she searched for a job that she liked the look of, but that didn't mean that he shouldn't take an interest in it.

She smiled at him.

"Oh, you know."

He realised that actually, no, he didn't. He had no idea what a volunteer at a hospital did.

"So what is it that you actually do?" he asked. "I mean apart from sitting by patients bedsides and holding their hands?"

Molly laughed.

"We soothe their fevered brows and then we carry a lamp around and sing hymns."

"No, really," said Jeremy. "Tell me what you do."

He was, he realised, genuinely interested. There was a life outside Sir Franks and he oughtn't forget it.

"It depends," said Molly, taking a sip from her glass. "It's all quite organised. We have shift managers who are also volunteers and they decide what people do on particular days. Sometimes I help to deliver mail or flowers, occasionally I'm in the shop. Today I was on meet and greet."

"Blimey. Sounds like air stewards."

Molly laughed.

"Nothing so glamorous. Basically it just means being on hand to show people where the various departments are. Hospitals are big places and they can be quite overwhelming. Sometimes we have a little chat with people if it looks like they need it. Which they sometimes do," she added.

"What do they want to chat about? Not their ailments, surely?"

"They do occasionally, you'd be astonished at some of the things that people tell you. But really it's more often the partner, the person who's brought them in, who wants to talk. They're worried and anxious and I guess some of them think that because we're associated with the hospital we're somehow part of the medical teams."

"So what do you say to them?"

"I explain that I'm not medically qualified and then usually I just let them talk. Sometimes I suggest they write their questions down so that they're prepared when they see the consultant or whoever. And that they take their phone in with them, so they can record the conversation. That's if the consultant will agree, which they usually do. In fact I think that these days the BMA encourage it," she added.

Jeremy nodded. That made sense. When people were frightened or confused they often got muddled or couldn't recall what had just been said to them. When one of the kids had come running into school the other morning and collided with him in the corridor, having just witnessed a car accident, he had been completely unable to describe what had happened other than to say that it had made a loud noise.

"I heard about a really sad case this morning, though," Molly continued. "One of the other volunteers told me. It happened last night. A fairly young man. His wife was brought in dead. The volunteer found him wandering around one of the corridors looking for the way out."

"What happened to his wife? Was it a heart attack or something?"

"No, a freak accident. He discovered her and called an ambulance but it was too late."

"So what happened?" he repeated.

"Apparently she liked to take a bath in the evening and when he realised that she had been up there for quite a long time he went upstairs to see if she was all right. It seems that she had some kind of fainting fit in the bath or something and drowned."

Jeremy felt himself go cold.

"I don't suppose that you know what her name was?"

Molly shook her head.

"No, the other volunteer didn't say. But she did say that she was a teacher."

CHAPTER TWELVE

Jeremy stood on the raised dais and watched as the pupils filed in. When he had reintroduced weekly assemblies it had been in the hope that they would help to pull the school together and foster a sense of belonging. Unlike the daily assemblies of his own school days, they didn't involve hymn singing and prayers. They did however include short reflective talks, news on the school sports teams, and celebration of any achievement by pupils or staff.

He knew that some of the staff thought that they were a waste of time and energy. But then some of the staff thought that any initiative was a waste of time and energy. In the event, and in spite of the gloomy predictions from what he was beginning to think of as the negativity squad, the assemblies had proved to be surprisingly popular. After a shaky start when a number of kids gave it a swerve while they had a fag round the back of the gym, most now attended. It had brought quite a lump to his throat when a large number of them had given a spontaneous rousing cheer when informed that the deputy head of history, Mr Anstruther, had won a silver cup at a local bowls competition. What had gone down particularly well was the special, longer monthly assemblies which were presented by the pupils themselves and often included popular music and snippets from social media.

What he hadn't foreseen was that he would need to use an assembly to break the news to them of the death of a teacher who, despite having been with them for such a short time, had proved to be surprisingly popular. Although it had happened over twenty-four hours ago the news hadn't already spread, he knew. There had been no shocked faces or whispering in the corridors, but it was only a matter of time. By midday, using the invisible antennae that teenagers often possessed, one of them would have picked it up and it would have spread through the school like wildfire. He thought it better that he should tell them all now, with the minimum of fuss, before any of them had the chance to embellish what was already a gruesome story.

He thought back to the previous evening while he waited for the pupils to finish elbowing each other and find their places. With a sinking heart he had rung the hospital. After establishing who he was and some whispered conversation, somebody somewhere had confirmed that the next of kin had already been informed. He had then waited for what had seemed like an age until the hospital had finally told him that the deceased young woman was Clarissa Ingram, former teacher at Sir Frank Wainwright's. And then he had abandoned the barbecue and driven over to the Ingram's house, thanking God that he hadn't had time to take more than a couple of mouthfuls of mojito. He wasn't sure exactly what he'd say when he got there but he could, at least, offer the condolences of the staff and pupils of Sir Franks.

The door had been opened quickly by a youngish attractive man, who Jeremy assumed was Rissa's husband. He had ushered Jeremy through to the sitting room and gestured for him to sit down. For a moment they had faced each other in silence. It was Jeremy who had spoken first.

"Mr Ingram, I'm so terribly sorry about your wife. We shall miss her enormously at Sir Franks. Although she had only been with us a short time, we all felt that she had made a tremendous contribution."

Dean Ingram had nodded.

"Thank you. Please call me Dean." He cleared his throat and stared down at his hands for a moment before looking up and speaking again. "Rissa was very happy at your school. There wasn't a day when she didn't look forward to going in."

Which was, thought Jeremy, more than you could say for most of the staff. Himself included on one or two occasions.

"Although," continued Dean, a small frown rippling across his brow. "I don't know, somehow she hadn't seemed quite herself lately. She seemed a bit distant, as though she had something on her mind. When I asked her if anything was wrong, she just said it was nothing, and not to worry. I didn't push it. I just thought, whatever it was, she'd tell me when she was ready. And now she never will be..." He tailed off and fell silent again.

Jeremy thought about what Dean had just said. Had Rissa been different lately? He didn't think so, but then he didn't see her every day. And Sir Franks did have an inspection looming in the not too distant future, so maybe Rissa was worried about that. If so, he wouldn't be surprised. They were all worried, and with good reason. Sir Franks had been given an Ofsted grade of 3 after the last inspection, which carried the tag of 'requires improvement'. Which was an understatement if ever he'd heard one. Anyway, whatever Clarissa had been worried about, there was no point in pursuing it. Poor Dean had enough to contend with without beating himself up any further.

"I'm sure that it wasn't anything important." He spoke

gently, hoping to reassure the younger man. "Otherwise she would have told you."

But would she, he thought. He didn't always tell Molly everything. Not because he had secrets from her but because he didn't want to worry her. Like that time he couldn't find his passport just before they were due to go on holiday. She hated flying and had already been stressing about it; he didn't want to make her feel any worse. Anyway, it had turned up as he knew it would. It was in the inside pocket of a jacket that he'd worn the last time they'd been abroad, along with a stash of Euros that he'd forgotten about. Which, as he thought later, was a bit of a result.

Dean nodded.

"I expect you're right." He paused and swallowed, raising his head slightly and blinking before speaking again, his speech suddenly bursting from him in a salvo of words. "I still can't believe it. I just can't. It seems unreal. One minute she was here and the next she was gone. I keep thinking that she's going to walk through the door any minute. Her school bag is still packed in the hall."

Jeremy had noticed it when he came in. A blue canvas bag with little wheels attached, it was stuffed with exercise books with the Sir Franks logo stamped on them. Rissa had obviously brought a stack of marking home with her. He would, he supposed, have to ask Dean for their return at some point. But not today. Instead, he fell back on the age old question.

"Is there anything I can do?"

It was the sort of thing that people always asked, he knew, but he meant it. He hadn't known Rissa for very long, but he had liked her and he would give assistance to her husband in any way that would be helpful.

Dean shook his head.

"I don't think so. I should have contacted the school this

morning, I know, but I just couldn't." He paused. "I haven't even told her parents yet. I haven't told anybody. I've just been sitting here all day, thinking about her."

Jeremy nodded in sympathy. He could understand that. It was as though, if it wasn't spoken of then it hadn't happened, a bit like children closing their eyes in the belief that it made them invisible. But Dean would have to tell Rissa's parents, and quite soon. There were arrangements to make. Dean looked at him and gave a faint smile, a far-away expression in his eyes.

"We met by pure chance, you know. There was some kind of demonstration on in London, I forget what it was about, and I got caught up in it. I'd gone to see an exhibition and when I came out, the streets were full of police and people shouting. The police were doing that kettling thing, you know, where they sort of crowd people together and surround them. I got swept up along with the rest. Rissa was demonstrating and she was shoved in next to me and we just started talking. I don't normally talk to strangers but there was just something about her..."

It was true, thought Jeremy, there was. It was difficult to put his finger on exactly what it was but if there was such a thing as quality of goodness, Clarissa Ingram had it.

"She had just come back from doing some voluntary work abroad and she told me about it," continued Dean. "It was really interesting." He smiled suddenly. "In fact so interesting that when the police let us out, we went for a drink. We started seeing each other and then we got married soon after. It was what we both wanted, there didn't seem to be any point in waiting. We got married in a registry office with just a couple of witnesses. Afterwards we had a pizza and a bottle of wine and that was it. That was the thing about Rissa, she hated a fuss."

He stood up and walked over to the window. For several

moments he stared out, hands in pockets, before turning back to face Jeremy.

"She came from quite a rich family, you know. Her parents were loaded and she was an only child. They had her late in life and they gave her everything. Private schooling, tennis and pony club, all that stuff."

Jeremy nodded.

"I guessed as much."

"She had a big trust fund, too, from her grandparents. But she never made a thing of it, if you know what I mean. She hadn't touched it. She said that she was keeping it for the right cause, something charitable. She hadn't decided what that was yet, but she said she would know when she found it. The truth was that she could have had more or less anything she wanted, but she just wanted to live like everybody else. And I did, too. It's what we both wanted and so that's what we did. She did like clothes though, I must admit that. But even those she saved for and waited for the sales. The same with shoes."

Jeremy had felt his shoulders relax slightly, he hadn't realised how tense he was. Dean had continued talking, the words that had probably been building up all day flowing over him in a gentle stream. He had felt his mind drift to what he needed to do to sort things out at Sir Franks. Get her classes covered, to start with. And then think about a permanent replacement. It seemed harsh but, in the words of the cliché, life had to go on.

CHAPTER THIRTEEN

Jeremy tapped in his password and stared at the screen. The assembly had been even more difficult than he had anticipated. While explaining that a dreadful accident had occurred and that Mrs Ingram was no longer with them, a number of the pupils had started crying. He had already informed the staff of her death before the assembly, but on hearing the news again, some of them had started to look distinctly watery-eyed as well.

Holding his own composure with some difficulty, he had finished by telling them that although Mrs Ingram would be sorely missed, they must all carry on and do their best. Because, he had added, it was what she would have wanted. It was interesting, he thought, how those remaining always knew what dead people would have wanted, usually when it coincided with what they themselves wanted. But in this instance it was, he was sure, true. Rissa had wanted to improve the prospects of their pupils. She had been determined to get the best out of them, and she would have wanted them to achieve something in their lives.

He jumped as his mobile suddenly blasted out 'The Birdie

Song'. Bloody Carlos. He really must change the pin on his phone. What if it had gone off during the assembly? He smiled. It was funny though. He glanced down at the screen. Chloe Kennedy.

Jeremy looked up at the big clock on the wall. If she didn't come soon, he would have to go back to school. He had a governor's meeting this afternoon and he needed some time to prepare for it, especially as Gerald Crawley would be in attendance. He felt a sudden flash of irritation. That damned man had done nothing but attempt to undermine him and give him grief since he'd taken up the post of head teacher, and he showed no sign of easing off. God alone knew how he'd come to be appointed as a governor in the first place, probably a crony of somebody, but he was exactly the sort of self-important busybody that shouldn't be allowed anywhere near a meeting of the local allotment society, never mind a meeting of school governors.

He wouldn't mind the criticism so much, he thought, if Crawley ever offered anything positive. Instead he just sat there, eating all the best biscuits and pointing out the cracks in the school's already crumbling façade. God knew what he was going to make of Clarissa Ingram's death. He'd probably take the opportunity to carp on about Sir Franks' failure to retain staff.

Behind the counter Alfonso carefully polished his new espresso machine. He looked, Jeremy thought, a bit downcast. Not like his usual self. In fact, while one could never accuse Alfonso of being taciturn, he hadn't given his usual cheery greeting to any of his customers today, merely nodding instead and taking their orders without speaking.

"I'm sorry I'm a bit late, sir. Mr Goodman, I mean," said Chloe, as she slid into the chair opposite him. "Only Maddie, she's one of the team leaders, asked me to run some stuff over to the post room before I took my lunch break." She pulled a face. "I don't like going over there. None of us do."

Jeremy smiled.

"Why not?"

"The man that works in there, Michael. It's the way he looks."

Jeremy didn't bother to ask her what she meant. He could tell from the expression on her face.

"So what did you want to see me about?"

"It's Ava," said Chloe.

"Who?"

"Ava. She works with me. She's a bit older than I am, she's my mentor."

"Right."

Jeremy suppressed a groan and resisted the urge to look up at the clock again. Surely to God Chloe hadn't got him here just to tell him that she had a mentor called Ava because, fascinating though that might be, he had a thousand and one other things to be getting on with.

Chloe lowered her voice slightly.

"She's had a letter."

Jeremy leaned forward. He was interested now.

"An anonymous letter?"

Chloe nodded.

"She showed it to me. She found it in her pigeonhole."

"What did it say?"

Chloe flushed.

"I don't really want to say, Mr Goodman." She hesitated and then continued. "It wasn't very nice though."

"Was she upset?" Stupid question, he thought. Of course she was upset. Who wouldn't be?

"She was really angry, I mean like furious. She said that she was going to the police." There was no mistaking the note of admiration in Chloe's voice. "She was asking around the office if anybody else had one."

"What did you say?" asked Jeremy.

"Nothing. Because if I said that I'd had any, they might want to see them."

"What about Miss Bates?"

"She's off sick. I mean, like long-term."

"What's the matter with her?"

Even as he asked the question he knew the true answer, whatever her doctor's note might say. If his and Chloe's guess was correct and Miss Bates had also received an anonymous letter, then presumably she was staying off work so she wouldn't get another one.

From behind them came the sound of a discreet cough. Turning, Jeremy looked up at Alfonso.

"I am sorry to disturb you, Jeremy. But I overheard what you and the young lady were talking about. Would you mind if I sit down?"

"Feel free." Jeremy pulled back the chair next to him. Alfonso sat down and passed a hand across his forehead.

"I think that you are talking about what I believe are called poison pen letters?"

Jeremy nodded.

"That's right. Why? Don't tell me..." he trailed off and stared at Alfonso. No wonder Alfonso had been so quiet today.

"Yes, I have received one. It was left in the café toilet. I am sorry to say," he turned apologetically to Chloe, "that I am relieved I am not the only one. I thought it was just me."

Jeremy resisted the urge to ask him to describe the contents of the letter. Alfonso was clearly suffering enough and whatever was in the letter, he would suffer even more if asked to repeat it in front of Chloe. But, he suddenly realised, if Alfonso had received one, then this was a breakthrough of a kind. Alfonso's café was directly opposite the town hall. Surely some of the employees came in for coffee and a sandwich at lunchtimes?

"Alfonso, do you know how many people from the town hall eat and drink here?"

Alfonso looked thoughtful.

"I am not sure. There are some, I know, because I see them through the window when they come down the town hall steps and cross the road."

"Are they regulars?"

Alfonso nodded.

"Most of them. Not all."

"Do you know any of their names?"

"Some, yes. Others, no."

Jeremy thought for a moment. It wasn't much, true, but it was something. Whoever was leaving the letters in the town hall also used Alfonso's café. At least it narrowed the field down a bit.

CHAPTER FOURTEEN

Jeremy dragged his gaze away from the local paper that Gerald Crawley had slapped down on the table, although it was difficult to ignore. The screaming headline said it all. Local Teacher Dies in Tragic Accident was blazoned across the front page. He listened as Gerald Crawley asked yet again whether Clarissa Ingram had been under any particular stress, which would, he pointed out, be no surprise to anybody given the challenges that Sir Franks posed.

Jeremy hardly had time to draw breath before Crawley waded in again. What, he wanted to know, were the school's safeguarding policies in relation to staff? What measures had been taken to ensure that new teachers were properly supported? How had the situation with Clarissa been allowed to develop?

Jeremy cleared his throat.

"I think that you're in danger of forgetting, Gerald, that Clarissa Ingram's death was the result of an accident. In fact, she was very happy at the school. Her husband told me so himself."

Gerald Crawley picked up another chocolate biscuit and slid it whole into his mouth.

Ignoring Jeremy's statement, he continued. Sure of the sound of his own voice, his arrogance seeped from every pore.

"What are the arrangements for mentoring new staff?"

The other governors sat in silence. If only, thought Jeremy, one of them would stand up to Crawley. He was a classic bully who had flourished under the previous interim heads, who had doubtless humoured him, knowing that, for them, he wasn't a long-term problem. Jeremy had no intention of doing any such thing himself. Crawley wasted hours of governors time and he was, frankly, a nuisance. He had thought long and hard about ways of getting rid of him but it wasn't as easy as he had first supposed.

The most usual way to get rid of a governor was if they failed to turn up to meetings, but there was fat chance of that. The man was always the first through the door. And there was no suspicion of any untoward activity in his private life, or none that was obvious. Besides, it seemed undignified to go trawling through a man's past in the hope of grubbing up some dirt. Also, if he was honest, who didn't have something in their past that they wouldn't want to see the light of day? It didn't necessarily make them bad people.

He looked at Crawley now. There was no denying that he was good-looking in a fleshy kind of way, but there was something repellent about the man. He was married, he knew. God pity his poor wife. Imagine waking up to that every morning.

He drew breath and squared his shoulders. Tragic though Rissa's death was, there was little more to say about it. There were more pressing matters to discuss, such as formulating the school policy on cyber-bullying. He made a show of shuffling the papers in front of him.

"Shall we move on?"

———

Jeremy watched from his office window as the last of the governors cars pulled away from the car park. He breathed a sigh of relief. Thank goodness that was over. Until the next one. But he'd really have to find a way of sorting out Crawley. The other governors had hardly been able to get a word in edgeways before he started talking over them, and he had particularly wanted their input on the issue of cyber-bullying. Some of the governors had teenage children and would almost certainly have something of value to offer. Of course, according to Crawley, it was all a fuss about nothing. Something blown up by the media to frighten the masses and sell news stories. While there might be a grain of truth in that, it was far from the whole story. From what Jeremy had read lately, cyber-bullying was both real and rife and its insidious influence got in everywhere. Of course, Crawley had suggested nothing positive but, after dismissing the whole idea as nonsense, had then pressed Jeremy for detail on his proposed policy, which at this stage he didn't have.

He turned back from the window and picked up the newspaper that Crawley had left behind. The details of Clarissa's short life spilled across the page. Her teaching, her voluntary work, her desire to fund a charity, it was all there. Presumably they had interviewed Dean Ingram, or maybe her parents. He looked up as his door opened.

"Visitor for you, Jeremy." His secretary pulled a face. "A police officer."

Jeremy groaned and dropped the paper back on the table. One of the kids in trouble. Or even worse, a whole gang of them. That was all he needed. First Crawley and now this. This was showing all the hallmarks of not being a good day. He crossed the room and sat behind his desk.

"Show him in."

He felt a pleasant sense of surprise as DC Renshaw, clad immaculately in suit and tie, entered the room. He stood up and held out his hand.

"Hello, good to see you again."

DC Renshaw took the chair indicated and, leaning down into the small black leather case that he had brought in with him, pulled out a tablet. Jeremy watched, interested. Did this mean that the day of notebooks was over? It would be a shame if it was. There was something very British about the sight of a policeman pulling a notebook from his top pocket.

"I was going to ring you," DC Renshaw said. "But I had another call out this way, so I thought I'd drop in on the off-chance."

"It wouldn't be about a young woman called Ava, would it?"

DC Renshaw gave a half-smile.

"Well, I know that news travels fast but that's pretty damned speedy. Who told you?"

"The girl who received one of the anonymous letters I showed you. She heard about it at work this morning."

"Right. Well, Ava called in to see us a couple of hours ago. She showed us the letter that she'd been sent. It was left in the same place as the others, in the staff pigeonholes. The inspector knew about the letters that your youngsters had received so he handed it to me." He laughed suddenly. "I'll tell you what though, our anonymous letter writer has picked on the wrong one this time. Given half a chance she'd hang, draw, and quarter him. With her own bare hands."

Jeremy grinned.

"She wasn't frightened then?"

"Not in the slightest. Just very, very angry."

"Good for her," said Jeremy. "Did she show you the letter?"

DC Renshaw nodded.

"She did. Here, have a look at this."

He tapped at the tablet and spun it round. Jeremy leaned forward and peered down at the screen.

Jeremy sat back, unable for a moment to speak.

"It's imaginative, I'll give it that," he said at last. "But why? I mean what on earth does the writer get out of it?"

DC Renshaw shrugged.

"Who knows? Some kind of power thing or something, I guess. A pity about that young teacher of yours," he added.

"Clarissa Ingram?"

"Yes, we got the shout the night before last."

Jeremy looked puzzled.

"Why? I mean it was an accident..."

"First and foremost, it's an unexpected death so we have to be notified. Basically, we have to consider it to be suspicious until it's identified as being otherwise. Whenever something like this happens, it's the first rule of the game. ABC."

"ABC?" repeated Jeremy.

DC Renshaw smiled again, a full smile this time.

"Assume nothing. Believe nobody. Challenge everything."

"Blimey. Sounds a bit like breaking up a classroom fight. So what did you find out? Or can't you tell me?"

"There's not a lot to tell really, and it will be in the public domain soon enough anyway. Obviously, we spoke to Mr Ingram. According to him he and Mrs Ingram had pretty much of a weeknight routine, and that night was no different. They had a few drinks together after dinner and then she went upstairs and had a bath before bed, which she did most evenings. After a while, he couldn't hear her moving about so he went upstairs to check that she was all right. He knocked on the door a few times and called her, but she didn't answer. She hadn't locked the bathroom door so he went in."

"And found her there?" asked Jeremy.

DC Renshaw nodded.

"Her medical records showed that she had been prone to fainting fits at one time. So on the face of it, it appeared that she'd had some kind of relapse in which she temporarily lost consciousness and slipped under the water. Obviously, we had a look round, but the scene was exactly as Mr Ingram described it, and that was confirmed by the ambulance crew who attended. There were no signs of a struggle. Staff at the mortuary were of the opinion that there were no physical signs that it was anything but an accident. But of course, given that it was an unexpected death, there'll be a post-mortem."

CHAPTER FIFTEEN

Aubrey glanced across at Vincent as he sauntered off across the gardens, intent on some business of his own no doubt, and then draped himself along the top of the wall. He liked it up here, you got a good view of the surroundings and the wall was just wide enough to accommodate him at full stretch. He watched as Jeremy bit into a huge steak burger and then wiped his chin with a paper napkin. It was interesting how they did that dabbing and wiping thing. He couldn't see the point of it himself, especially when you could lick it off later and enjoy it all over again. He laid his chin on his paws. It didn't look like there'd be much chance of leftovers this evening, not like the last time when Jeremy had suddenly rushed off, and Molly and Carlos had been left with a pile of uneaten chicken kebabs and griddled prawns. Now that was what he called a result. But you never knew, and there was no point in wasting an opportunity. He jumped down and parked himself next to Carlos. If anybody cracked and gave him a little something it would be Carlos. He washed his ears and watched as Carlos flipped two more steak burgers. He'd been rather quiet this evening, Aubrey thought.

Perhaps something had upset him, he didn't seem like his usual cheerful self.

"So how was your day, Carlos?" asked Jeremy. "Anything interesting happen?"

Aubrey felt a sudden change in atmosphere. Sensing it too, Jeremy leaned forward.

"What is it, Carlos? What's the matter?"

Carlos shrugged and kept his back turned as he busied himself with a bowl of salad.

"Nothing."

Molly tipped her head to one side and studied him for a moment.

"Has something happened at work? Has somebody upset you?" She paused and then continued. "Jeremy told me about the nasty letter you were sent. Have you had another one?"

Carlos turned to face her and nodded. He swallowed and ran his hands down his striped apron before speaking.

"Yes."

"Was it left in the same place?" asked Jeremy.

Carlos nodded again.

"Yes, in my pigeonhole."

"Have you still got it?"

"It's in the car. Do you want me to go and get it?"

Molly, Jeremy and Aubrey watched as Carlos loped round the side of the house. Molly turned to Jeremy.

"He's obviously upset."

"I'm not surprised." Jeremy's tone was grim. "I dread to think what our dear poison pen has come up with this time."

"Are you going to show it to the police?"

Jeremy nodded. "I have to. This business is getting out of hand. Honestly, Moll, you should have seen the letter that the girl Ava was sent. It was pure filth..."

"Shh." Molly laid a warning hand on Jeremy's arm. "He's coming back."

"Here."

Carlos handed a sheet of white printing paper to Jeremy and sat down. Jeremy read it in silence and then handed it back. Carlos passed it to Molly and then suddenly jumped up from his chair, his face scarlet.

"It's not true, Jeremy. Honestly, I swear. Molly, you know it's not true. I've never had any diseases. But if this goes round then everyone will say that I have and then they'll stop coming into the restaurant because nobody will want food prepared by me and then I'll lose my job and I'll never get another one." He paused for breath and then continued, his voice passionate. "And I'll never have my own restaurant. I'll never be a famous chef. It'll be the end of everything."

Molly and Jeremy exchanged glances.

"It's all right," said Molly, her tone soothing. She patted the chair next to her. "Of course we don't believe it."

Carlos sat down again and sniffed back the tears.

"I didn't know it was called that. I had to look it up. And that stuff about me stealing money..." he paused and stared down at the ground.

"What?" said Jeremy.

"Some money did go missing from one of the restrooms. Somebody left their handbag in there. Everyone was talking about it."

"But, Carlos, nobody will seriously think..." began Jeremy.

Carlos tightened his mouth.

"Yes, they will. That's what they'll all think. Because I'm the newest one there. Nothing went missing before I got there, you can see for yourself, it says so in the letter. And," he added bitterly, "I'm the youngest. I'm the easiest to blame."

He had a point there, thought Aubrey. In the cat world it wasn't the youngest that got scapegoated, on the basis that none of them was exactly sure how old they were, but it was generally the littlest. Like that time Moses got the blame for tipping off the cats over the railway bridge that Rupert and Roger were planning a surprise attack. Moses didn't even know where the railway bridge was, let alone be able to make his way across it. Aubrey's money was on Lupin, whom he had long suspected of being a double agent. He settled himself down to listen as Molly, Jeremy and Carlos continued talking. He had a feeling that there was more to come.

As if sensing that too, Molly leaned forward and looked at Carlos more intently.

"Carlos, is there something else? Something that you haven't told us?"

Aubrey glanced up at Carlos. Molly was right. He could see from the expression on Carlos's face that he was holding something back. For a moment Carlos remained silent as if deciding whether to speak or not. When he did his voice was low and hesitant.

"This morning I found a blue scarf in the car park." Carlos hesitated and then continued. "Somebody must have dropped it on their way in. Anyway, I put it in my locker and then I forgot about it until after lunch. When I remembered, I went to the pigeonholes. There's a lost property pigeonhole where you just put in anything that you find and then whoever's lost something can go and check it. It's usually just keys and stuff like that."

Carlos stumbled to a halt and looked away.

"And?" asked Jeremy.

He turned back, his face doleful.

"I saw Jamal."

"The head chef?" asked Molly.

Carlos nodded and swallowed.

"The thing is, he'd already checked his pigeonhole this

morning. He said so because somebody had left some food thing magazines that he likes in there and he showed them to me. But when I saw him there this afternoon he looked really guilty. He had his back to me and he jumped when I spoke to him, and then he sort of rushed off. Afterwards, back in the kitchen, he hardly looked at me."

"So do you think it might be Jamal that's writing the letters?" Jeremy asked.

"I don't know. But why else would he be hanging around by the pigeonholes? And why did he look so guilty? But I don't want it to be him. I really like him."

And that, thought Jeremy, was yet another consequence of these damned letters. Not only did they cause distress to those that received them, it also put everybody else under suspicion. And in so doing so caused irreparable damage to relationships. He stood up and pulled his phone from his pocket.

"I'm going to call DC Renshaw. If he's not there I'll leave a message."

Carlos stood up, too. The note of panic in his voice was unmistakable.

"You're not going to tell him about Jamal? It's probably not even him. I only told you what I saw. Please, Jeremy, don't tell the police."

"Don't worry, I'm not going to tell him about Jamal. But I am going to tell him that you've received another letter. This damned business has got to stop before somebody gets seriously hurt."

CHAPTER SIXTEEN

J eremy hauled Aubrey off the windowsill and settled him on his lap while he mulled over the events of the previous evening. He and Molly had finally managed to reassure Carlos and eventually he had gone up to his room. He hadn't gone to bed though, they had heard him moving around up there and every now and then the faint murmur of his voice had drifted downstairs. He had, Jeremy was certain, been talking to his girlfriend Teddy.

He thought about Teddy for a moment. He hadn't been particularly certain of her at first. A very pretty girl from a well-off family with a number of obvious advantages in life, he hadn't been at all sure that she would be good for Carlos. If he was honest, he had been afraid that she would soon get bored with him, that the novelty of having an orphaned Brazilian boyfriend whose mother had been murdered would wear off and she would revert back to the privileged posh boys that she was used to, leaving Carlos with a broken heart. But he'd been wrong. Teddy and Carlos had been together for over two years now and there was no sign that their relationship was weakening. If anything, it had grown stronger despite her living so far away.

In any event, the chat with Teddy had obviously done some good because this morning Carlos had been full of beans. Apparently, he and Teddy were planning a day out somewhere, perhaps by the seaside, maybe somewhere like Brighton. Carlos hadn't mentioned Jamal again. Neither had he said anything when he'd come home this afternoon, other than to say that it had been a hectic day. Apparently it always was when it rained. Nobody wanted to go out for lunch and so they all piled into the town hall restaurant. So much so that Jamal always checked the weekly weather forecast so he could adjust for it. Jeremy had been glad of the poor weather today, it meant that Carlos had been kept so busy it gave him less time to think. Apart from the horrible accusations in the letter he had received, it must have turned the knife even more at the thought that it might be Jamal.

Ever since Carlos had started working at the town hall he had talked about Jamal. How kind he was, how clever he was, how everybody liked him. The thought that Jamal, somebody whom he admired, would be capable of such acts would be devastating, as Jeremy knew only too well.

When he was a teenager there had been a lad named Karl whom they had all thought was the epitome of cool. Whatever Karl wore, they all tried to copy. Whatever music Karl was into, they were too. They had all looked up to him. When it had been reported in the local press that he had been charged with several indecent assaults, Jeremy and his friends had been appalled. Not only at the fact that Karl had been engaging in such shocking behaviour, but that they had all aspired to be just like him. Karl's habit of deliberately sitting uncomfortably close to girls on buses and grinning around at his mates had just seemed like Karl messing about at the time. Viewing it with an adult eye, he saw it in an entirely different light now.

He wondered what had become of Karl. Given the current

understanding that so-called low-level sexual offences were often the gateway to more serious matters, it was highly likely that he was in prison with the added qualification of sex offender on his CV. Could it be possible that Jamal was a similar Jekyll and Hyde character?

He'd looked Jamal up earlier on Facebook. As expected, Jamal had a page. His image had showed a warm, friendly, attractive man, smart in his chef's whites, smiling as he tucked into a bowl of something. He hadn't given any personal information about himself, but that didn't really mean anything. Not everybody shared everything. According to his profile his main interests were golf and history. If he had any other interests, they weren't mentioned. Although, Jeremy reflected, writing obscene and unkind letters to colleagues probably wasn't the kind of thing he would want to advertise.

He had stared at the image long and hard, as if he could gain some insight by doing so. But no matter how long he looked at Jamal's photograph, it was practically impossible to reconcile the image of the smiling chef with the writer of the letters. Although the same might have been said of Karl, the good-looking popular teenager with a sideline in perversion. He found himself suddenly wondering if, in spite of being a chef himself, Jamal ever visited Alfonso's. He might well do. Being surrounded by his own food all day, he might enjoy escaping from a busy kitchen and having the relative luxury of eating something that someone else had prepared. He must remember to ask Alfonso the next time he visited the café. Jamal was quite distinctive. If he was a customer then surely Alfonso would remember him.

He set Aubrey down on the floor and poured himself another glass of wine. He ought to cut down, he knew, but tonight he just didn't feel like it. It had been a tough day at school and he needed to relax. An aggressive parent had managed to barge her way onto the school premises by using her son's entry card and had made straight for his office, like some kind of vengeful homing pigeon.

According to her, Sir Franks were completely failing her son by not supporting him. What support the boy required she didn't seem to be sure about, just that he needed it and he wasn't getting it. He had responded by quietly pointing out that the boy in question was hardly ever in school, as evidenced by the Year Nine registers that he had been looking at only that morning, and the fact that his mother was in possession of his entry card clearly indicated that he wasn't in school that day either. These prolonged and unexplained absences, he said, did make it rather difficult for the school to carry out an assessment to find out what was required. He'd eventually managed to get rid of her, but her anger had hung in the air and the encounter had taken it out of him, as well as eaten into an already crowded day.

And of course, the kids were still upset about Rissa, which was hardly surprising. He had finally managed to get hold of a supply teacher, a young earnest looking man with heavy spectacles and trousers that were slightly too short, but he wasn't feeling optimistic. There was something about him that just invited trouble. Like sharks sensing blood in the water, the pupils at Sir Franks could smell weakness a mile off. But Jeremy was the beggar that couldn't be the chooser and he just prayed that the supply teacher wasn't having too hard a time.

Rissa had been well-liked and the pupils would undoubtedly resent any replacement. He took another mouthful of wine and forced himself to switch his thoughts from school in an effort to relax. He hoped that Molly would be back from the hospital soon, he hated it when she did these twilight shifts. And Carlos wasn't here either, he'd gone back to work to help out with the catering and serving for a group of Danish visiting dignitaries for whom the council were throwing a reception. There was, he thought, something very melancholy about sitting on your own at seven thirty in the evening.

He didn't feel like reading and there was nothing worth watching on the television – he'd already wasted ten minutes flicking through the channels. It was weird, he thought, when he was a boy there were only three channels but in his memory there was always something to look forward to. He'd read somewhere only the other day that in the 1960s the prime minister of the day, Harold Wilson, had successfully persuaded the BBC to change the broadcast time for *Steptoe and Son* on election night because he was afraid that the voters wouldn't turn out while the programme was on. Much chance of that happening now. These days there were what seemed like hundreds of channels and nothing that he wanted to view. He turned his head as Molly came in.

"Glass of wine?"

Molly dropped her handbag on the floor, sat down on the sofa, and leaned back.

"Yes please."

"Hold on, I'll fetch another glass."

Aubrey strolled into the kitchen after him and sat on his foot as he reached into the cupboard. There might be the possibility of a little something. He wasn't hungry but a food opportunity was a food opportunity. Jeremy smiled down at him.

"Aubrey, don't you ever get bored with eating?"

Not really, thought Aubrey. He watched as Jeremy reached into the cupboard for another glass and then followed him back through to the sitting room. It had been worth a try.

"I found out something at the hospital this evening," said

Molly as Jeremy poured a glass of wine and handed it to her. "Something about that young teacher of yours that died. Some of the volunteers were talking about it."

Jeremy topped up his own glass and sat back down.

"What was that?" he asked.

"They've done the post-mortem."

Jeremy sat forward, interested.

"And?"

"They're saying that it wasn't an accident. They're saying that she took some kind of overdose."

Molly had gone up to bed and, unlike earlier, he was glad to be alone now. Her news had been a bit of a shocker, to say the least, and he wanted some quiet time to think. He'd known of course that there would be a post-mortem, DC Renshaw had told him that. And really he shouldn't have been surprised that it had happened so quickly. He wasn't entirely sure what a post-mortem involved but it was obvious that it would have to take place sooner rather than later. It wasn't the kind of thing that could be left indefinitely. It was unpleasant to think about, but he had assumed that it would just be a necessary formality.

He knew from Rissa's personnel file that she was, or had been, subject to fainting fits and it had seemed clear that she had suffered one while in the bath. What had never occurred to him was that there might be some other cause. But an overdose? It was incredible. Why would a lovely young woman like Rissa, with her whole life before her and everything to live for, have ended it?

He had never known anybody that had committed suicide, not really. There had been a boy when he was at school, but that boy had been several years older than him and Jeremy couldn't even remember his name. Nor could he remember anything else about him. Just that the head master had informed the school of the poor boy's demise and had advised the pupils not to discuss it and not to dwell on it. And they hadn't. Thinking back now, he suspected that the whole thing had been so alien to him that he hadn't wanted to think about it and neither had anybody else.

But Rissa, of all people. He would have said that she was about the least likely person to do such a thing. But how could you tell? When he was in sixth form he had studied *King Lear* for A level and the image of the poor wretch wandering on the heath with the desperate plea to 'let me not be mad' had stayed with him over the years. It had, he supposed, pretty much set his template for mental illness when he was young, but he knew now that it was very far from the reality. People with mental health problems were, in most respects, just like everyone else. Except in extreme cases, there was nothing to mark them out as being different. A mind in turmoil wasn't visible like a broken leg or arm.

He ran his conversation with Rissa's husband back through his mind. Dean had said that Rissa hadn't seemed her usual self of late, and he had obviously been right. He felt a sudden rush of guilt. He should have noticed. He should have done something, he should have tried to help her in some way. But even if he had known that she was troubled, what could he have done? Realistically, short of locking Rissa in his office and demanding that she talk to him, he knew there wasn't anything.

He turned as Aubrey sidled into the room and jumped onto the arm of his chair. Leaning across he ran his hand over his thick fur.

"What do you think, Aubrey?"

Aubrey looked at him and then settled himself more

comfortably. It had been a trying couple of days. What should have been a nice family barbecue with himself getting the leftovers had turned into a bit of a drama, and now there was Jeremy and this post-mortem thing. Frankly, he could do without thinking anything. There was enough thinking going on in the world without him adding to it.

CHAPTER SEVENTEEN

Jeremy hesitated and then leaned forward and pressed the bell one more time. It was a difficult visit but one that he had to make. If Dean wasn't at home, then he would just have to come back another time. He should, he realised, have asked for his mobile number when he saw him the last time but it hadn't occurred to him. The only number that he had on record was Rissa's and, even supposing that the battery hadn't gone flat by now, he could hardly ring that. It seemed that the Ingrams, like many people, had dispensed with their landline altogether. But in any event, somehow or other he had to get the exercise books back. It would have been monumentally insensitive to ask Dean to bring Clarissa's school bag into school, but he couldn't just leave it where it was. The kids had been very good about not asking for the return of their work, but he was aware that one or two had started to raise it and he knew that he couldn't put it off for much longer.

He glanced up at the windows. There was no sign of life that he could see. Perhaps Dean had gone away for a few days. He wouldn't be surprised, given everything that had happened. He turned to make his way back down the path, when the front door was suddenly pulled open. Dean Ingram stood in the doorway, his face pale and his chin unshaven. Jeremy could see over his shoulder that the canvas bag was still exactly where Rissa had left it. He stood awkwardly for a moment, not sure what to say. He should have thought this one through a bit more.

"Come in," said Dean, and stood back to allow him entry.

Jeremy hesitated. Presumably Dean knew the results of the post-mortem by now and if he didn't, then he didn't want to be the one to tell him. All he really wanted was to pick up the bag and leave.

"No, it's fine," he said. "I don't want to bother you. I just wanted to collect the exercise books. I'll be out of your way in a moment."

He felt a sudden urge to just step away from the front door and make for the car. He wanted to be away from the cloud of death and at home with Molly and Carlos, watching television, with Aubrey and Vincent tucked up between them. It was selfish, he knew. On the whole, his was a happy and fulfilling life and here was Dean Ingram alone and grieving. And to make matters even worse, his grief had just been compounded by the post-mortem results, or was very shortly about to be. Not that Jeremy could say or do anything to make matters any better. He remained silent. It was better to say nothing than to stick his fingers in the wound.

"Please," said Dean. "Come in. I wanted to ask you something."

Reluctantly, and with a sinking heart, he followed Dean through to the sitting room. Was Dean going to ask him something to which he had no real answer? Well, he supposed he could listen, even if he had nothing sensible to offer in return. He owed Rissa that at the very least. He sat down on the sofa and waited.

"I suppose you've heard?" Dean spoke softly, his face expressionless.

Jeremy nodded. There was no point in pretending that he didn't know what Dean was talking about.

"They were mine, you know."

Jeremy looked at him, confused. What was his?

"The sleeping tablets," Dean continued. "They were mine. Our doctor prescribed them for me ages ago when I was having a bit of trouble sleeping. I didn't take them for long, just a few nights, and then I shoved them in a drawer. I'd forgotten all about them. Rissa must have found them."

Dean sat down heavily in the chair opposite and dropped his head into his hands. Jeremy leaned forward.

"Dean, you weren't to know."

Even as he said it he could hear how lame it sounded. But what else could he say? Anyway, it was true. While Dean had suspected that Rissa was disturbed about something, he could hardly have anticipated that she would take such drastic action. Dean dropped his hands into his lap and looked up, his expression doleful.

"I should have. I should have seen the signs."

"You mustn't be so hard on yourself. Dean, this is not your fault."

Dean stared at Jeremy, his expression blank.

"It wasn't the first time, you see. She'd tried it before. She had a breakdown when she was a teenager, did you know?"

Jeremy felt astonished. He had assumed that whatever had troubled Rissa was recent. He'd had no idea that she had a history of mental health problems. There was certainly nothing in her records about it. It was hard to believe. Rissa had always seemed so level-headed and unruffled.

"No, I didn't know that."

Dean gave a wry smile.

"Not many people did. Her parents hushed it up at the time. They didn't want anybody to know about it. They thought it was something to be ashamed of. They never spoke about it, they still deny it even now. It happened when she was about fifteen. They sent her to some place in Ireland. A convalescent home or something. I doubt if it's even on her medical records."

"But she told you?" Jeremy asked.

Dean nodded.

"Yes, she told me. We both agreed that we shouldn't have any secrets from each other."

Which was how it should be, thought Jeremy. He didn't have any secrets from Molly. Well, only things like that time he'd put diesel in the car instead of petrol and had to have the engine drained. And he was pretty sure that she deliberately didn't tell him how much she paid to have her hair done, which was just as well. He had a distinct feeling that if he knew, he might faint clean away. But by and large they had always been open and honest with each other.

For several moments the two men sat in silence. In the distance the sound of the church clock striking the hour hung in the air. Some people in the town didn't like it, Jeremy knew, but he did. There was something gently reassuring about the deep solemn chime. But it reminded him that time was getting on and he still had other things to do.

"What was it that you wanted to ask me?"

Dean cleared his throat and swallowed, as though steeling himself to speak.

"There's going to be a coroner's inquest and it seems likely that I'll have to give evidence. That's what I wanted to ask you. Will you come with me?"

Jeremy's heart sank as he pinned what he hoped was a reassuring smile across his face and nodded.

"Of course."

What else could he say?

Jeremy thought about what he knew of Coroners' courts as he drove home. His experience of the legal system wasn't great, but he did know something about Coroners' courts. He had been one of the people who had discovered the body of Carlos's mother, Maria, and as such had been required to attend the inquest to give evidence. Of course, the other person who had found her had been Carlos, who had returned home to find her dead body and then run off into the night.

The coroner had been very gentle with Carlos and had taken considerable trouble to explain to him that it was not an adversarial process, but simply an inquiry to establish what had occurred. They weren't there, she had said, to assign blame or undertake any criminal investigation. They were just there to gather the essential facts, to try to piece together what had happened. The whole process had been much quicker and more efficient than he had imagined and afterwards he had taken Carlos for a pizza. They had sat and eaten their meal in silence, each lost in their own thoughts and both relieved that their ordeal was over.

The only other courts that he'd been in was the Crown Court when a friend of his who was studying law had taken him to see a murder trial, and the youth court when he felt it necessary to support one of Sir Franks number. If he was truthful, he had found the Crown Court quite boring, especially as he hadn't really understood the issues under discussion. But a Coroners' court wasn't that kind of court. They didn't argue points of law or try to catch people out. It was an official inquiry into the circumstances surrounding a person's death and they were generally held when a person's death was violent or unnatural.

While Rissa's death hadn't been violent, it had definitely been unnatural. He had tried to reassure Dean that there was nothing to be anxious about, but he wasn't sure that Dean had been convinced and, really, he didn't blame him. Of all the things that you might expect to experience in a lifetime, giving evidence at your wife's inquest probably wasn't one of them. But as long as Dean could hold it together he would be all right, he was sure. Anyway, he didn't have much choice. He'd been summoned as a witness and that was that.

Jeremy parked the car and reached across for Rissa's school bag. He had been tempted to leave it in the car ready to take into school the next day, but it would be just his luck that this would be the night that his car was stolen. He pulled the bag out. It was bloody heavy, just as well that it had wheels attached. He lugged the bag upstairs to his study and dropped it on the floor. Strange to think that the exercise books that Sir Franks used were not that much different to the ones that he had been issued with when he was at school. No doubt many would consider them old-fashioned, and on the face of it they were, but it was all very well people insisting that schools and colleges do everything electronically, the fact was that computers cost money. At Sir Franks they had a number of laptops and tablets but not enough for every pupil. And when it came to homework, quite a few of the kids didn't have access to a computer at home. It was true that most of them, if not all, had mobile phones, but there was a limit to how much work you could expect them to produce on a phone screen. Additionally, computers blew the doors wide open on opportunities for cheating and plagiarism. So for now Sir Franks was, like many other schools, still partly reliant on the good old-fashioned exercise book.

He glanced across at Aubrey who had just slipped round the door after him, and then dipped his hand into the bag. Drawing out a book, he flicked through the contents. It was interesting. Rissa had obviously set some pieces of work based on the popularity of so-called influencers and had posed some really quite challenging questions for the pupils to answer. This particular pupil had made a pretty good stab at answering them, even using selected quotes to illustrate a point. He smiled to himself. It was a bit more innovative than the kind of essay that he had been set when he was at school, which more often than not ran along the lines of 'what I did on my holidays'. He reached down and drew out another book. The contents of this one were different, presumably it was from another class. He'd better sort them out and he might as well do it now as wait until tomorrow.

Leaning over, he grasped the bottom of the bag and shook out the contents. He stared down at the books now spread out over the floor and felt suddenly unbearably sad. In years to come these pupils would remember Rissa as that teacher who died. They would remember that about her, long after they'd forgotten what she looked like or what she had taught them. He straightened up again and stretched. He still hadn't decided if he was going to break the news about the results of the post-mortem to them although, of course, it was entirely possible that most of them already knew. He wouldn't be surprised. Although he hadn't heard any mention of it so far, it didn't take long for news such as this to spread and Sir Franks had an underground network second to none. And then there were the staff to consider as well.

He sighed and rubbed his hand over his forehead. What he needed was a breath of fresh air to help him think straight. Turning his back on the books, he walked across the room and opened the window. Leaning out, he breathed in the fresh autumnal air. He liked this time of year, in fact he preferred it to the spring. When he was at school, September had meant different teachers and new exercise books, crisp afternoons on the playing fields, and walking home from the bus stop feeling the first fresh chill blow across his face. Even now, it seemed that autumn was about hope and new beginnings. The hot dusty dog days of summer were gone and the earth was swept clean. It was a time to start again and make new plans, a time when anything might be possible. Except for Rissa. She would never make any plans now.

He turned back from the window, and felt his heart thud against his chest. The canvas bag was moving. He stood transfixed with horror, his mouth dry, watching as it inched towards him. A fat furry paw reached out and tapped him on the foot. He grinned.

"Aubrey, you little sod. Get out of there. Come on."

Reaching into the bag he tucked his hand under Aubrey and began hauling him out, and then stopped. There was something else in the bag, something caught in the seam. He tugged it free and drew it out.

CHAPTER EIGHTEEN

Jeremy looked around him as he waited for Dean to give his evidence. The inquest was being held in one of the courts sited in the grounds at the back of the town hall. A high-ceilinged baronial building, built in the gothic style, it had originally been the old Assize court, but now served as the Crown Court and sometimes, as on this occasion, the Coroners' court. It was easy to imagine some poor wretch in here, up before the beak, cowering in the dock and totally overwhelmed by his surroundings. Some of them would have been, literally, children.

He knew that before Victorian times no distinction had been made between criminals of any age and he'd read that there were records of children as young as twelve being hanged for what these days would be seen as quite trivial offences. He shivered slightly. It was a horrible thought. If they'd lived in those times half the kids at Sir Franks wouldn't have seen their thirteenth birthday.

He pushed the thought away and slid a glance across at Dean, who was looking worried, but resolute. According to DC Renshaw, he had taken the news about the letter found in

Rissa's school bag very badly, which was hardly surprising. No man would want to read that kind of thing about his wife. The letter had been particularly nasty, accusing Rissa of corruption and embezzlement during her voluntary work abroad, and of being over-interested in some of her pupils, most notably boys and girls in Year Eight. And that was the sanitised version, as Jeremy knew, having read it when he found it.

At first he had been puzzled as to how the writer of the letter had known not just that Rissa was a teacher, but about her voluntary work, and then he had realised. It was obvious. Social media. The destination to which all roads led. He'd been a bit late to that particular party himself, but had quickly learned that was how everybody found out things about other people these days, and the younger they were the more likely you were to find them.

With the advent of Facebook, Instagram and the like, people's lives had become open books. You could discover all sorts of things about almost anybody without having to leave the comfort of your own home. He'd flipped open his tablet, opened the app and, sure enough, there she was. Scrolling down he found the image of a smiling Rissa in among a group of other volunteers as they set off on their adventure, followed by pictures and posts during their time away. He'd scrolled back up to more recent pictures of her wedding day.

Standing outside a grim looking civic building with road works clearly visible in the background, Rissa and Dean had held hands and smiled into the camera of whoever was taking the photograph. Rissa, dressed in a blue cotton summer dress, looked impossibly young and Dean, in his smart chinos and open-necked shirt didn't look much older. Dean had been right when he had said that she hated a fuss. If it hadn't been for the captions beneath the images, he would never have guessed that it was their wedding day. She wasn't even holding any flowers.

Would Dean want to remove the pictures, he wondered. And if he did, was it even possible? He didn't have a clue but he did know that if it were him, he wouldn't be in too much of a hurry. While the images were still there, some part of her would still remain, it would feel as if she hadn't quite left. To take them away would feel too final. But of course more pressing than whether or not Dean would remove Rissa's Facebook page was the question of how the poison pen had selected her as a victim and had then managed to get his disgusting letter to her? As far as anyone was aware, the centre of operations was the town hall with Alfonso's café as an outpost, so to speak.

He sat quietly while he thought about it, and then it dawned on him. Of course. Rissa had visited the town hall when they had taken the kids to the careers fair. And not only that, the town hall had been provided with a list of names in advance and they had been given pre-prepared name badges to wear. Presumably Rissa had been picked at random from the list by somebody who had access to it. Having checked out the possibilities on Facebook or similar, the poison pen must have thought she would make the perfect target. Young, attractive, and successful, in his nasty resentful little mind she must have seemed ideal material for taking down a peg or two.

He felt suddenly more optimistic. If the poison pen had access to the list of delegates to the careers fair, then surely that narrowed the field. Or did it? Carlos had told him that when the Danish dignitaries had visited, notice of their visit had been posted in advance in the weekly electronic newsletter, along with all their names. Presumably then that was the case with all external visitors, including those attending the careers fair. Well, not necessarily all the pupils, but certainly the names of their schools and the staff accompanying them. The newsletter went to all staff, so potentially several hundred people had seen it, which opened up the floor again. But presumably they hadn't all been at work that day and of those that had, they hadn't all dropped in to the careers fair.

Some town hall employees had taken a look, he knew, because Carlos had told him. In fact Carlos himself had called in and had waved to him from across the room. The letter writer already knew what Rissa looked like from social media, so all he would have to do was sidle up to her and drop the letter in the canvas tote bag they had all been given and which most of them had worn slung over their shoulder.

The fair had been crowded, it would have been easily done. Either that, or just leave it somewhere it would be seen, perhaps in the women's cloakroom. Even if Rissa herself hadn't gone in there, one of the pupils would and would have passed it to her. And if it had missed the mark, if the opportunity hadn't presented itself, it wouldn't have mattered. There were plenty of other people that the poison pen could target. But the opportunity had presented itself and it had hit the mark.

He pulled his attention back to the present as Dean was called to give his evidence. The man still looked very pale, but he had at least shaved, and was wearing a suit and tie, as was Jeremy. He watched as Dean took the stand, his voice low but clear as he answered the questions put to him, describing his last evening with Rissa, measuring out every detail including what they'd eaten for dinner and what they'd talked about. Jeremy felt a sudden constriction of his throat as Dean paused and swallowed, his voice faltering as he started to describe going upstairs to the bathroom. The coroner leaned forward and gave a reassuring smile.

"Take your time, Mr Ingram. There's no hurry. Please feel free to tell us anything that you feel may be relevant."

Dean nodded and briefly closed his eyes before speaking again.

The two men walked outside and stood together for a moment. Across the car park which the court shared with the town hall, Rissa's parents got into their car and drove off. Jeremy guessed that they were Rissa's parents as soon as he had seen them in the court. They had sat close together, almost huddled, as they listened intently, the grief evident on their faces. Rissa's mother had sat with her handbag on her knees, clutching at the straps throughout, her knuckles white against the strain. Her father had simply stared woodenly ahead, his mouth clamped shut as though to stop himself from suddenly crying out. Jeremy had wondered whether he ought to go over and introduce himself afterwards but had decided against it. They were clearly suffering and looked as though they would prefer to be left alone. He would write to them instead, presumably Dean had their address. Dean watched the tail lights of their car disappearing and then turned back to face Jeremy.

"It wouldn't have killed them to at least say hello." The small lines around his mouth tightened. "They never liked me. They thought I wasn't good enough. They wanted something along the lines of a high court judge, or a doctor or solicitor at the very least, not some dreary little man in finance. And they were furious about the wedding. They were all set on a big church affair with hats and hymns and a huge reception in some stately home. They wanted to put on a show to their friends and neighbours. If that was what Rissa had wanted, then of course I would have gone along with it. But she didn't. She actually told me that she couldn't imagine anything worse." He paused. "I don't think that they really knew their daughter at all."

How many parents do, thought Jeremy. He'd lost count of the times at parents evenings when the child under discussion seemed to have undergone a personality change every time it entered the school gates. But it seemed so tragic that in this time of loss and sorrow that Rissa's parents couldn't have at least offered Dean some comfort, and he them.

"I don't suppose I'll see them again," said Dean. "Apart from at the funeral, of course."

At the thought of the funeral Jeremy's sense of relief that the inquest was over faded a little. He hadn't asked Dean about the arrangements yet, but it would obviously be in the not too distant future. Some of the pupils had already been asking about it and he suspected that quite a few of them would like to attend. He'd been turning over the possibility of shutting the school for a half-day. It would be easier all round if he did, given that many of the staff would attend the funeral too. No doubt he would have to get permission from someone, but he couldn't see it being refused.

"Anyway, I don't care," Dean continued. "I shan't be here for much longer. I'm going to sell up. I've thought about it and I've decided. I'm going away. There's nothing for me here now."

Jeremy nodded and resisted the urge to advise him not to do anything too hastily. Presumably, Dean knew his own mind and perhaps it was for the best. The modest little house that he'd shared with Rissa stood as a permanent reminder of their life together and, of course, there was Sir Franks. It was a requirement that pupils wear school uniform, a school tie at the very least, and most of them did. The fact that some of them chose to tie it as a bow or wear it wrapped around their head didn't alter the fact that it was a clear emblem of their belonging. Every time Dean saw one of them larking about in town while they bunked off lessons or fighting at a bus stop on their way home, it couldn't fail to remind him of Rissa.

"Where will you go? Have you got somewhere in mind?"

Dean shrugged.

"I'm not sure. I haven't decided yet. I don't think it matters, not really."

Jeremy rather thought that it did matter. Dean Ingram was still young. He had a life ahead of him, albeit not the life that he had planned, and at some stage he was going to have to start living it. It wouldn't do for him to take himself off to some remote part of the country with only sheep and seagulls to talk to. But who was he to give advice? He wasn't in Dean's position and he hoped to God that he never would be. Anyway, it wasn't really any of his business. The immediate future was going to be difficult for Dean and there was no easy way to deal with it. He would just have to get through the best way he could.

"I thought that I could maybe travel for a bit," Dean continued. "While I think about it."

Jeremy nodded.

"That might be a good idea."

And on the whole he thought that it might. At the very least it would be a distraction. He realised suddenly that he didn't know what Dean did for a living other than something in finance but, again, he was fairly young, a career break probably wouldn't hurt him. In fact, in the circumstances it was entirely understandable.

"Well, I'll be going now." Dean paused. "Thank you for coming with me today, I appreciated it."

Jeremy watched as Dean climbed into his car and drove off. In all, he considered that Dean had handled himself well. He had given his evidence clearly and concisely and even when the evidence of the anonymous letter was introduced by DC Renshaw he had remained calm. It had, Jeremy reflected, been particularly horrible to hear the letter read out in court. He had noticed the clenched fist of Rissa's father and the downcast eyes and flushed neck of her mother as the obscene contents were relayed for them all to hear.

As he listened, he had wondered, not for the first time, why Rissa had kept the letter in her school bag. Surely her first instinct would have been to destroy it. Perhaps she had meant to show it to somebody, maybe even report it to the police. But then again, perhaps her fragile mental state had left her confused and afraid until she became overwhelmed and she hadn't known what to do. She hadn't told Dean about it either and he wondered why not. She had read it, he knew, because the envelope which had contained it was opened. In any event, the coroner had been vehement in his denouncement of the harm that the writers of such letters did and the verdict, or conclusion as the coroner called it, had hardly come as a surprise. He had appeared in no doubt that, given the circumstances and in the light of Rissa's past struggles with her mental health as described by Dean, Rissa had intended to commit an act that had resulted in her death.

He looked around him at the half-empty car park. It had that desolate air of late afternoon when the best of the day has gone and the evening hasn't yet started. He wasn't sure what he wanted to do now. It wasn't quite four o'clock but he didn't want to go back to school and, anyway, he didn't have to. It was one of the perks of being the head teacher that the only person he had to answer to was himself. But although he didn't want to go back into school, he didn't really want to go home either. Carlos would still be at work, and Molly was volunteering so the house would be empty. Probably even the cats would be off out on some business of their own.

He leaned against his car while he thought about the events of the afternoon. Like the inquest into Maria's death, it had all gone more smoothly than he had feared. There had been no huge surprises. Everybody there more or less knew what was coming. Apart from Rissa's parents, he supposed. They probably hadn't known about the letter. It must have been the most dreadful shock. He felt suddenly desperately sorry for them. All the trouble that they had taken to hide Rissa's disturbed mental state, only to have it all dragged out in public now. Although, he reflected, perhaps if they had been a bit more open about it years before then it may not have come to this.

He felt suddenly ashamed. He was being rather harsh. Rissa's parents had only been trying to shelter her. Dean had told him that they had Rissa late in life. They were from a different era – an era when mental illness carried a real stigma and one which they feared she would bear throughout her life. No doubt they had done what they thought was right at the time, just as most people do.

In fact that had been the most poignant moment of this afternoon's proceedings, when Dean had turned to the pathologist who had been called to give evidence and asked if she thought he could have saved his wife if he had gone upstairs earlier. It was a question, of course, to which there was no real answer. The coroner had nodded at the pathologist, giving her permission to answer. She had given the only answer that she could, namely, that it wasn't possible to know. And with that Dean had to be content. Although no doubt, thought Jeremy, it would be a question he would continue to ask himself for years to come.

He looked down at his watch. Alfonso's was only across the way. He could do with a hot coffee and a slice of Alfonso's delicious chocolate cake. He shook the handle of his car to make sure that it was locked and then turned towards the road. Beetling across the car park at the other end a familiar figure bustled into view. Jeremy stared. It was Gerald Crawley. What on earth was he doing here? He hadn't been at the inquest that was for sure. Apart from the fact that he had no reason to be there, Jeremy would have noticed him. And the only other users of that part of the car park were town hall employees.

CHAPTER NINETEEN

J eremy sat back and let out a sigh of exasperation. Nothing in any of the digital files that he had inherited contained anything about the background or appointment of the governors. But such information must exist, he was certain. They hadn't just appeared from another planet, although in the case of Crawley that was a possibility that couldn't be entirely discounted. He looked around him and then paused as his eye lighted on a big grey metal cabinet in the corner of the room. Of course, the filing cabinet. It stood as a battered testament to the days when everything was recorded on paper. It was never used now, in fact apart from a brief glance inside he hadn't opened it since he took up office. He kept meaning to have it removed. But if records weren't to be found digitally, then the most likely bet was that they would be in the filing cabinet.

He jumped up and crossed the room. Pulling open the top cabinet drawer, he tugged out a slim cardboard folder. Flicking it open he felt a surge of disappointment. All it contained were receipts for some building work that had been completed five years ago and a booklet of tickets for free school meals. The latter had long been redundant, with those pupils eligible simply tapping their phone or card on the reader in the dining hall. He reached down and pulled open the second drawer. The contents of this one looked more promising, containing as it did records and minutes of governors meetings, but still no details of the governors themselves. He pulled open the bottom drawer without expectation of finding anything more interesting than some old sports day posters, but he was wrong. Right at the back, behind some screwed up sheets of paper, lay the file that he wanted.

He carried it back to his desk and pulled it open. Spreading the documents out, he looked at them with interest. The application forms that the governors had been required to complete prior to appointment were all there and contained a positive wealth of information. Who would have thought, for instance, that Jane Lucas had been a county swimmer in her youth? No wonder she was so insistent that timetable allocation for games shouldn't be reduced. And he'd had no idea that Tom Groves had not only worked for some time as the manager of the local theatre, but was also the author of a number of books about the environment.

He had, he realised, not been using his governors to full effect. He had been so preoccupied with the daily grind of firefighting that he had totally failed to recognise the assets that were in front of him. There was a positive gold mine here in terms of knowledge and experience. To be fair to himself, part of his lack of recognition was, he knew, due to Crawley's dominance. Crawley had the hide of a rhinoceros and resisted all attempts to shut him up. The result was that he had, very early on, come to view governors meetings as not much more than a necessary nuisance. He shuffled the papers in front of him until he found the ones he was looking for. Gerald Crawley.

Senior administrative officer. Place of employment, the town hall.

He sat back as the thoughts crowded in on him. Crawley worked at the town hall. Crawley also knew Rissa. Well, not personally, but he would have been aware of her appointment. Was it possible, could it be, that he was the writer of the poison pen letters? Jeremy was sufficiently self-aware to acknowledge that he wouldn't be sorry if he was. All right, it would be bad publicity for the school, but given the reputation that Sir Franks already had that wouldn't be too much of a consideration. Besides, they'd ridden out worse. Such as the time a group of boys and girls had decided to celebrate the end of exams by drinking vodka in the park. The resulting carnage had been spread all over the front pages of the local paper. The irony had been that at least half of the miscreants hadn't bothered to turn up for the exams anyway. Although, he supposed, on the plus side they had shown a certain collegiate spirit.

But if Crawley was outed as the poison pen it would not only mean that the letters would stop, but he would get him off the board of governors permanently. And then there was the added bonus that Carlos would be relieved that it wasn't Jamal. He smiled to himself. It was almost certainly wishful thinking. He disliked Crawley intensely, a sentiment in which he was fairly sure he was not alone, but that didn't make the man a criminal, much as he would like it to. It did, however, put him on the list.

He swept the papers back up and pushed them to one side. He would ask his secretary to digitise them when she could find time. In the meantime, he had other work to do. He flipped open his laptop and stared at the screen, conscious that he was having trouble focusing properly. Yesterday the inquest had taken it out of him, more than he had thought it would, and it had furthered disturbed him that Alfonso's had been closed. In all the years he had been visiting Alfonso's he had never known it to be closed before the stated time. But yesterday the blinds had been pulled down and the closed sign turned uncompromisingly towards the street.

CHAPTER TWENTY

Aubrey, Vincent and Moses strolled round the corner and made for the café's side entrance. It had been some time since they'd visited Muriel and they were all looking forward to seeing her. There was something very wise and restful about Muriel, and they felt the need of it today. Everybody seemed so jangled lately. Even Carlos seemed to have a permanently anxious expression.

Slipping easily through the cat flap they stopped and sniffed the air. Usually there was a sense of hustle and bustle about the place, a clatter of crockery and the hiss and gurgle of the coffee machine. This morning there was an eerie silence. Aubrey turned to Vincent.

"Something's up."

Vincent nodded. They padded quickly through the swing door to the front of the café. The blind was down and there was no sign of Alfonso. They turned as Muriel approached.

"Where is he?" asked Vincent. "Is he all right?"

Muriel nodded.

"Sort of. He closed early yesterday and he hasn't opened since. I think he's depressed."

Aubrey and Vincent looked suitably solemn and after several seconds Moses followed suit. None of them were sure what being depressed was, but from the look on Muriel's face it wasn't anything good.

"It means he doesn't feel very happy," explained Muriel.

Aubrey thought about it. This sounded serious. Alfonso was always happy. He didn't think that he had ever seen him less than cheerful. Nothing seemed to get him down for long, not even that time Muriel had told them about, when there'd been a power cut and a whole oven full of baking went in the bin. Alfonso had just started again and still managed to have some cakes and biscuits ready for opening time. In fact Aubrey had often thought that he and Alfonso could be related. Well, they could be if Alfonso was a cat. But now he thought about it, Alfonso had been unhappy the last time he'd visited as well. Muriel had told him that he'd been off his food and it had been because he'd had one of those letters, the same sort that Carlos had. That was the trouble with this reading business, he thought. It sort of followed you round. Like, literally.

"Has something happened?" he asked. "Has somebody upset him?"

Muriel nodded.

"He's had another letter. He found it yesterday when he went to check on the toilets. He always checks them regularly in case anyone has left a tap running or something and he checks them even more now, since he had the first letter. Anyway, he found it and after he'd read it he closed the café and went to bed. He's been there ever since."

All four cats turned as Alfonso came through the swing door and walked slowly towards them. The strings of his big apron, striped in the green, white and red colours of the Italian national flag, hung loose and his skin was tinged with grey. Aubrey glanced sideways at Vincent.

"He don't look too good," said Vincent.

That, thought Aubrey, was putting it mildly. Alfonso looked dreadful. They watched as he released the catch on the blind, making it rattle swiftly upwards, and then sat down heavily on one of the pine chairs. Reaching down he scooped up Moses and settled him on his lap and then stroked the top of Aubrey's head. Aubrey let out a loud purr. While he wouldn't normally purr on so slight a show of affection, he felt that today Alfonso needed it. Given how often Alfonso had slipped him and Vincent scraps of tuna and cheese, it seemed like the least he could do.

Alfonso gave a long, slow, weary sigh and rubbed his hand across his eyes.

"I suppose today that I must carry on as usual. I must pretend that nothing has happened." Alfonso looked down at Moses who was now fast asleep, and spoke slowly, as though each word cost him an effort. "It is not the fault of my other loyal customers that one of them is the apple gone bad. Because if I am not open, where will Mr Woodruffe go for his afternoon tea? I must not be selfish."

Aubrey agreed. He knew Mr Woodruffe, by sight at least. They all did. A small man, a former school teacher by profession until his mental health had made it impossible for him to continue, with very clean, pink skin and wispy tufts of grey hair combed neatly down on his almost bald head. Mr Woodruffe visited Alfonso's twice a week after he finished his part-time voluntary work archiving material at the town hall. He dressed in a suit and tie even on boiling hot summer days and always carried a raincoat over his arm which he placed carefully on the chair next to him. He rarely spoke, other than to say please and thank you, although he had once helped Alfonso fix his computer. It had, as Alfonso had explained to Aubrey and Vincent, gone completely bonkers so that he was unable to retrieve any of his accounts. And as he ordered most of his ingredients in bulk and online, it was a disaster. Mr Woodruffe had refused any sort of payment, but Alfonso occasionally slipped a big piece of cake into a paper bag and gave it to him to take away, saying that it was a gift for his wife if Mr Woodruffe would like to take it. Mr Woodruffe invariably did like to take it and would give a small shy smile of thanks. He reminded Aubrey of his old friend Mr Telling, of whom Aubrey had been very fond. He didn't know if Mr Woodruffe had a cat but he would put money on it, if he had any, that he did.

And it wasn't only Mr Woodruffe who relied on Alfonso's café, he knew. The small residential school down the road regularly booked in groups of their students and Alfonso always rearranged the tables and chairs so that those in wheelchairs could get them in. Aubrey liked those students. There was something free-spirited about them. They always enjoyed themselves, particularly as Alfonso would put together a selection of cakes and biscuits and arrange them on the tables for them, and they often wrote him little illustrated thank you letters afterwards which Alfonso displayed on the counter. Where else would these students go for tea and cake if Alfonso's was closed? They weren't welcome in some of the other cafés in town, he knew, because he'd heard their tutors telling Alfonso about it.

"But what if it is Mr Woodruffe who is writing these damned letters?" Alfonso continued, his voice cracking now. "What if it is Mr Woodruffe who is accusing me of having mould on my food and rats running through my kitchen?"

Unlikely, thought Aubrey. But then you never knew. Mr Woodruffe was a frequent visitor to the café and he always used the toilets before he left. It could as easily be Mr Woodruffe as anybody else. He watched in alarm as Alfonso dropped his head to the table and his shoulders began to shake. He had hardly ever witnessed a grown-up cry before, although he'd seen Carlos cry after his mother had been murdered. Alone and upstairs in his bedroom, hunched up on his bed with his back to the wall and his hands pressed to his face, Carlos had sobbed his heart out. At those times Aubrey had done the only thing that he could think of, which was to hunch up along with him in a show of solidarity until it was over. But he'd rarely seen a grown-up do it, certainly not Molly or Jeremy. There was something frightening about it, as though the order of the world was being disturbed. He gave a small sigh of relief as Alfonso raised his head again, his eyes still swimming. Alfonso reached into his apron pocket for a large white handkerchief and blew his nose.

"This is no good. I must not let this take over. I must not let it get to me. Whoever is doing this thing is perdente."

Muriel turned to Aubrey and Vincent.

"It means loser," she said.

Aubrey and Vincent nodded, impressed. Was there anything that Muriel didn't know? Alfonso sniffed and finished wiping his nose. Stuffing his handkerchief back into his pocket he looked around at the prints of Italian alps and gondolas which adorned the walls, and gave a faint watery smile.

Placing Moses carefully on the floor, Alfonso stood up and walked over to a small framed photograph which took pride of place in the centre of the prints. He stared at it for a moment and then turned to face the cats.

"This is my family. My father, my mother, my brothers and sisters. See the street where we are standing. That is Sorrento, where I was born. It overlooks the Bay of Naples and it is very beautiful."

Alfonso closed his eyes briefly and raised his face as though he could feel the warmth of the Sorrento sun again.

"Now this is my home and I do not want to leave. I have not made my fortune but I have worked hard and I am happy here. I have made friends and this is where my life is. It is where I want it to be." He smiled down at the cats. "I must not let some rotter take it away from me."

Aubrey gave an inward smile. Alfonso often used these strange expressions. He didn't know what a rotter was but it sounded good. He watched as Alfonso crossed the room and switched on the big coffee machine. The machine started a familiar hum as it began to pulse into life, followed by the comforting glug and gurgle of water heating up. It must mean that Alfonso was feeling a bit better.

"Alfonso, there you are. I've been worried about you."

The four cats and Alfonso all turned as a tall smiling figure made his way towards the counter. Alfonso raised his hand in greeting.

"Jamal, my friend. It's good to see you."

CHAPTER TWENTY-ONE

J eremy looked around him. It had been a long time coming
and the crematorium was full. All of the staff had turned
out, including the caretaker and refectory staff, as well as
most of the pupils that Rissa had taught. He was touched to see
how all of them had made an effort. More or less dressed in
school uniform and their ties, for once, tied properly around
their necks, they stood quietly at the back and whispered
together as they waited for the ceremony to start. He felt a
sudden start of alarm as each of them started taking their phones
out. Surely to God they weren't going to take pictures or start
texting or anything? But no, he'd misjudged them. Each of them
were turning their phones off and replacing them in their
pockets. They must have agreed beforehand that it was what
they would do. Given that their phones were, for most of them,
their lifeline it was a real mark of respect. He felt suddenly
inordinately proud of them. They'd done really well at the
special assembly, too.

It had been the idea of Rissa's tutor group to hold it and the
hall had been packed. Even the most diehard refuseniks had
deigned to put in an appearance, for once forgoing the

opportunity to have a fag break round the back of the gym. The tributes had been moving, with each speaker recounting a special memory which ranged from her reading aloud to them to her lovely laugh when one of them made a joke. Two of them had written poems which, although generally derivative of the-cat-sat-on-the-mat variety, had nevertheless been from the heart. They had finished with a song that was in the charts. Jeremy had never heard it, and he suspected that neither had most of the older staff, but it had gone down well.

They had also managed to obtain some photographs of Rissa which they displayed on the overhead projector as a backdrop and which Jeremy recognised from Facebook. How they had managed to obtain them he thought it was better not to ask. Rissa may have hated a fuss, but surely she would have been gratified at such a display of affection.

Dean Ingram hadn't attended, although obviously he had been invited. Jeremy didn't blame him. They had still been waiting for the funeral arrangements to be finalised and there was presumably only so much that the poor bloke could take. Rissa's parents had been there though.

Jeremy had been surprised at their acceptance. The kids had written out the invitations and he had suggested inviting them, more in hope than expectation. He hadn't for a moment thought that they would turn up. But he'd been wrong. They had accepted and taken their places as guests of honour at the front. He had watched her father smiling encouragement as the kids went through their set pieces and he realised suddenly how like her father Rissa had looked. She'd had the same tilt of the head when she smiled and the same soft blue eyes.

He'd invited them to his office for tea afterwards and, as he listened while they talked about their daughter, he realised that he'd pre-judged them. He had somehow imagined that they would be stiff and unyielding, that their desire to keep up appearances would always be paramount. Again, he'd been wrong. They were actually rather gentle. Still stunned from the death of their only child, they had talked softly about how proud of her they had been and how much she had achieved in her short life with her voluntary work and then her teaching. Of Dean, they had said not a word.

He looked at them now, sitting quietly together on the front row, waiting for the wicker casket to be borne in. They seemed to have aged, appearing even older than since he had seen them at the assembly. Presumably it was the weight of the grief they carried. At the assembly, they had done their best to be deliberately upbeat, they had tried to contribute towards the celebration of Rissa's life into which her tutor group had put so much work. Now, there was no need to wear a mask. Nobody needed to put on a show of being upbeat at a funeral, especially when it was the funeral of your much-loved only child.

Dean sat alone on the front row opposite, the seats either side of him empty. Presumably given his status as chief mourner, people had felt that they didn't have the right to occupy the same space. Like Rissa's parents, he stared straight ahead. They might as well have been in separate rooms for all they acknowledged each other, Jeremy thought.

Sitting in the row behind, among the staff from Sir Franks, was Gerald Crawley and two other governors who had clearly felt that it was their duty to put in an appearance. Behind them sat DC Renshaw. Jeremy straightened up as the vicar made his way to the front and cleared his throat.

Outside in the autumn sunshine, people stood about admiring the floral tributes and chatting quietly with each other. The service had gone well, Jeremy thought. The eulogy had been delivered by the vicar, presumably based on information supplied by Dean, and there had been only one hymn, the ever-popular "All Things Bright and Beautiful". It was, he knew, often despised by those who lived on a higher plane, but he liked it. It was one of the few hymns that most people were familiar with, having sung it at primary school, and therefore unlike some of the more esoteric numbers, it was one that people could join in with. Anyway, Rissa had been bright and beautiful, so it was appropriate in every respect.

He looked around him. Crematoriums were, by their very nature, not the most cheerful of places but this one had made a real effort, with neatly laid paths and attractive shrubs. Dotted here and there were little memorial benches for the bereaved to sit on and remember their loved ones. Situated on the outskirts of the town and away from the noise of the traffic, it had an air of peaceful stillness to it. There were, he thought, worse places to sit and think about lost friends and relatives. He watched as Dean, smart in his dark suit and black tie, spoke quietly to several of the mourners. Presumably they were colleagues of his or friends of his and Rissa's, they weren't staff at Sir Franks at any rate. Standing some distance from him, Rissa's parents chatted to her pupils.

He glanced away down the long drive. In the distance he could see another funeral procession making its slow way towards the crematorium. Clearly they'd had their allotted time and should be leaving. He'd better start rounding the kids up and getting them on the coach he'd organised. He was glad now that he'd raised the subject of the wake with Dean.

He'd been reluctant at first but it had been Molly who had wondered whether Dean had made any arrangements. She had suspected, correctly as it turned out, that he hadn't. It was understandable, really. Apart from the grief of losing his wife, and in such a dreadful way, he almost certainly didn't have much experience of these things and perhaps he hadn't even thought of it. Given his age, it was entirely possible that he hadn't ever attended a funeral. Unlike the Victorians and Edwardians, death was not woven into the fabric of most people's lives. Nevertheless he had been hesitant about making the offer to put something on and, again at Molly's suggestion, he had framed it as a tribute to Rissa from the school. He was pleased now that he had. People expected something and Alfonso would put on a good spread.

CHAPTER TWENTY-TWO

The little café looked bright and cheerful. In addition to the tables laden with sandwiches and cake, into which Gerald Crawley had already started making inroads, Alfonso had also opened the doors to the courtyard garden and placed extra tables and chairs out there. The last of the late roses tumbled over the walls making it, thought Jeremy, the perfect antidote to the sad proceedings of the morning. He made his way over to where Alfonso stood proudly behind the counter, ready to dispense tea and coffee as requested. He had offered to buy in wine and Jeremy had been tempted to agree but had in the end decided against it. The pupils from Sir Franks would be there and, while they had been as good as gold up till now, it might be a stretch too far to expect them to resist the lure of alcohol. Anyway, he and the kids and staff had to go back into school this afternoon and no doubt other mourners had jobs to return to.

He reached for the coffee which Alfonso handed him.

"You've done a grand job, Alfonso."

Alfonso beamed at him.

"Thank you, Mr Goodman. It is my pleasure. My friend Jamal helped me."

Jeremy turned to see a smiling man passing round plates of sandwiches. Carlos had mentioned that he would be in charge of preparing lunches this morning, this was obviously the reason why. Anyway, that answered one question. Jamal was clearly very familiar with Alfonso's café. He waited as Jamal put down the plate he was holding and approached him.

"You must be Mr Goodman. Alfonso has told me about you. Carlos has talked about you as well."

Jeremy felt surprised.

"How did you know it was me?"

Jamal's attractive face creased into a smile.

"Carlos told me that you're the head teacher at Sir Franks. Not many people arrive at an occasion such as this on a coach with a load of young people in school uniform."

Jeremy smiled back. Of course.

"Alfonso also told me about the dreadful letters that he has been receiving. A terrible business, Mr Goodman, terrible." He paused. "Ah, I see that you are in demand."

Jamal turned away as Rissa's parents approached Jeremy.

"Mr Goodman," Rissa's father spoke quietly, his soft blue eyes solemn. "Thank you so much for your letter, it meant a great deal to us."

Jeremy inclined his head slightly. There didn't seem to be anything to say to that. It had been a difficult letter to write. Handwritten letters, never mind letters of condolence, were not things that many people these days had much experience of composing. He and Molly had between them spent some time writing a number of drafts before they had been satisfied. They had in the end, he thought, managed to strike the right note by telling Rissa's parents what a loss to the school her untimely death was and how much they would all miss her, without being too mawkish or eulogising her to the point of incredulity. All too often, he felt, the deceased were given attributes that had somehow managed to go completely unobserved during their lifetimes, particularly when it came to younger people. He could understand it, such descriptions came out of love, but he wanted to avoid it in Rissa's case. She had been a lovely young woman, but she hadn't been a saint and, he suspected, nor would she want to be remembered as one.

"We also wanted to thank you for organising this," Rissa's mother waved her hand in the direction of the cakes and sandwiches. "We did offer to make the arrangements but Mr Ingram told us that it had already been taken care of." She paused and her face suddenly hardened. "Frankly, I'm surprised that he allowed us to attend at all."

Rissa's father smiled at his wife.

"I don't think he had the power to stop us, my dear, much as he might have liked to." He turned to Jeremy. "As you may gather, Mr Goodman, we are not on the best of terms with our son-in-law." He sighed. "Of course, he was not what we would have chosen for Clarissa..."

His wife interrupted him.

"There was a lovely boy. Henry. They met at the tennis club. He was a little older than Clarissa, he worked for an investment bank. We've known his parents for years. He and Clarissa were very close and we had great hopes. It would have been a most suitable match. That's not, I know, a very fashionable thing to say but it's the truth. But no, she had to go and meet Dean Ingram. At a demonstration of all things."

Her husband sighed.

"The trouble with Clarissa," he said. "Was that she was a dreamer. She was always going to change the world."

"It's a pity that she couldn't change Dean Ingram." His wife's bitter tone was unmistakable. Her eyes narrowed. "Do you know, Mr Goodman, right from the start, he resented us and he showed it. Nothing that we could do was right. We tried. We honestly did try, but it's very difficult with a man like that. We did our best not to mind too much about the wedding. Obviously it wasn't the wedding that we would have wanted but, after all, it was their day. We know that Clarissa wanted to invite us, she told us so, but apparently he persuaded her that at our age it was a long way for us to travel and, in his words, it was only about a piece of paper anyway. He told Clarissa that they could make it up to us later, invite us for a long weekend when they got the house the way they wanted. And that was another thing, we offered to pay the deposit on the house but no, he wouldn't have that. So then we offered to buy some furniture for them but he flatly refused that too. But the invitation to visit them never came." She paused and pressed her lips together for a moment before adding, "And now it never will."

Jeremy remained silent. This wasn't his quarrel and he suspected that there was probably right on both sides. Rissa had been her parents only child and it was natural that they would want to continue to be involved in her life. On the other hand, what young man wanted his parents-in-law hovering on the sidelines or, worse, having to be grateful for their largesse?

"We wrote and asked him for some of Clarissa's things," she continued, a slight tremor in her voice. "In particular a little teddy bear that she'd had since she was a small child. It went everywhere with her, even when she did her voluntary work overseas. He never even replied."

Clarissa's father turned away and swallowed before speaking. He turned back, clearly struggling to compose himself.

"Those things he said about her at the inquest. Not a word of truth in them. None whatsoever. Clarissa did go to Ireland when she was a teenager, it was the summer before her GCSEs and she wanted to spend some time with her cousins." He raised his voice slightly. "That's all it was. Just a visit to her cousins."

They were still, thought Jeremy, in denial. He remained silent as the other man continued, his voice lower now and his tone one of defeat.

"Anyway, what does it matter? Nothing will bring her back. What's done is done. I don't suppose that we shall hear from him again." He held his hand out towards Jeremy.

"We should be going now. It's a long drive back. Thank you once again for everything that you've done."

Jeremy watched as the couple gathered their things together and, studiously avoiding Dean, bade farewell to the other mourners.

CHAPTER TWENTY-THREE

Jeremy watched as the last of the pupils made their way out of Alfonso's café and began straggling their way back to school. At least, he hoped that they were straggling their way back to school and not straggling their way to some pre-planned mischief.

"Mr Goodman."

He turned as DC Renshaw, immaculately dressed as ever in dark suit and crisp white shirt, stood before him.

"It was a good turnout, don't you think?"

Jeremy nodded. "Very good. I guess that it usually is for a young person."

He hesitated for a second. This didn't seem the right moment to ask about the letters but he wanted to know what was happening. He'd received a text from Chloe Kennedy the previous afternoon to say that she'd had another one and she had sent him an image of it. It had been particularly nasty, referring to what everybody apparently knew went on in the Kennedy household once the curtains were closed. Clearly the writer of the letters wasn't going to be deterred by the tragic death of Rissa. If anything, from the tone of the last letter that had been sent to Chloe, he was ramping things up.

Jeremy cleared his throat and ploughed on. "I was just wondering, if in fact, well, whether…"

DC Renshaw gave a small smile.

"Whether we've got any further with the letters?"

DC Renshaw nodded.

"Since Clarissa Ingram's death it's certainly shot up the list of priorities." DC Renshaw glanced around him and over to where Alfonso was chatting quietly with Jamal. "Thank you for telling us about Alfonso. He was a bit reluctant to talk at first, in fact initially he denied it. I think he thought that he was in some kind of trouble. Anyway, in the end he showed us the letters he's received. Very unpleasant. But we've been giving it some thought and we've had a number of ideas."

Jeremy moved slightly closer, aware that Jamal was looking in their direction, and lowered his voice.

"What are you going to do?"

"Well, my first thought was covert cameras."

"Are you allowed to do that? I mean, is it legal?"

"In some circumstances, yes. One of those being prevention of a specific crime. It could be very useful in the pigeonhole area of the town hall, which is where a number of the letters seem to have been placed. Clearly we couldn't place one in Alfonso's toilets."

"How will it help in the pigeonhole area?" asked Jeremy. "Everybody uses them. Carlos told me that staff are expected to check them every day."

"That's the problem. Everybody has a legitimate reason to be there. Also, we'd have to get the co-operation of the chief executive, and he's already indicated that he's not keen on the idea. So, while we're not dismissing it altogether, we've had another thought."

"What?"

"Put somebody on the spot. Somebody that most people would barely register."

"Such as?"

"Some kind of maintenance person, somebody who would generally be around the building."

"But surely," said Jeremy, "he, or she, would be noticed."

"Not really," said DC Renshaw. "How often do you notice the site staff or cleaners around Sir Franks?"

Jeremy thought about it for a moment. It was true. Site maintenance generally did a good job but they were usually agency workers and they did come and go. Apart from the site manager, formerly known as the caretaker, who was a permanent employee, he'd be pushed to put a name to any of them. If asked, could he actually even describe one of them? On the whole, he thought not.

"After you told us about the letters," continued DC Renshaw, "I went and had a look. It's a bigger area than you might think. It's more like a small meeting place, really. It's got a few easy chairs and a coffee table, as well as a coffee machine."

Jeremy was surprised. When Carlos had talked about pigeonholes, he had imagined a small, dimly lit, dusty area tucked away at the back of the building, a nineteen-fifties post-war leftover from pre-digital and electronic days, somewhere people had left handwritten memos for their colleagues in the days when instant communication to the next office, never mind almost anywhere in the world, was the stuff of science fiction.

"So you'd just sort of hang about?" he asked.

DC Renshaw nodded.

"My boss took a bit of persuading at first, but when I pointed out that it was really a stakeout, just like any other, he agreed. I doubt it'll last though. There's a limit to how long he'll let me loiter around the town hall in fancy dress. But I suspect it will be easier than you might think," he added. "Put a pair of overalls on and nobody thinks about it."

Jeremy smiled. It was true. Acquire some kind of uniform and anything was possible. His father had once told him that, for a lark, when he was a young student he and a couple of friends had borrowed some white coats from one of their student doctor mates and had then proceeded to stroll around the local hospital. Not one person had questioned who they were or what they were doing, although they had, he said, pulled short of strolling into the operating theatres.

"You'll still have to get the go-ahead from the chief executive though, won't you? I mean you can't just walk into the building."

DC Renshaw nodded.

"He's already agreed. I met him when I went over there. Nice bloke. He didn't have a clue about the identity of the poison pen, but obviously he's anxious to put a stop to it. Preferably with as little publicity as possible."

"So how would it work? Could you record people on your phone?"

DC Renshaw smiled.

"Not really, no."

"Why not? People record stuff and take photographs on their phones all the time. Look at all the things that are posted on social media."

"It's okay to take photographs in a public space, but when it's private property it's a bit of a grey area. There are issues around privacy."

"Do the pigeonholes count as private property?"

"Well, yes. As in, the general public don't have access to them. We would need to ask permission and, obviously, if we asked permission it would defeat the objective."

Jeremy thought for a moment. He still couldn't see how this

would actually work. Presumably people came and went in that area all the time. How would a police officer know who they were or whether what they were placing in a pigeonhole was legitimate or not?

"Apparently," continued DC Renshaw, "most people are in the habit of checking their pigeonhole in the morning on their way into the offices. It's unlikely that the poison pen places the envelopes while people are milling around, so presumably he comes at a less busy time. Therefore, anybody that comes later in the day would be noticeable, particularly if they put something in one rather than just checking their own. I should be able to get a good view of him and we know what the envelopes look like, they're white with a printed label stuck on, so once that person has gone it would be easy to take a quick look in the pigeonhole to see what has been placed there."

"What about DNA?" Jeremy asked. "Can't you check the letters that you've already got?"

"Not as easy as you might think. DNA can be left on paper although fingerprints are better. The letters are at the lab now but there's quite a bit of backlog, it might be several weeks before we get any results. We've asked them to look particularly at the underside of the sticky address labels. They look like the sort that you peel off so it's entirely possible that some traces have been left there. But my guess is that our letter writer is almost certainly quite forensically aware."

Jeremy nodded. Lots of people, himself included, watched police investigation documentaries. You'd have to have been living in some sort of closed community not to be aware of things like DNA.

"So he'll have covered his hands?"

"Yes, which will be another way of spotting him when he puts a letter in a pigeon hole. In any event, I suspect that the only prints or DNA we'll find on the envelopes and the letters will be those of the people we know have handled them. Which reminds me, we would like to take yours and Carlos's at some point, for elimination purposes."

Jeremy suddenly felt strangely uncomfortable, although he had nothing to hide. Almost everything about everybody was already out there. He only had to search for something online before a slew of advertisements danced their way onto the screen, prompted by some algorithm or other. And it was frightening, or it would be if he allowed himself to think about it, how often filling in forms online took only a matter of seconds because the information required was already there. Anyway, uncomfortable with the prospect or not, he could hardly refuse.

"But," said DC Renshaw, "I'm not sure, at this stage, that any identification of DNA will take us much further."

"Why not? I thought DNA was the answer to everything?"

DC Renshaw pulled a face.

"If only. No, it's only really useful if we've got a match with somebody who's already in the system. Other than that we'd have to check the fingerprints and DNA of everybody who works at the town hall."

"So what's the problem with that?"

"Well, first of all it's voluntary. We can only request that people come forward to be tested, we can't insist, and it's not unknown for people to refuse on principle. And secondly the chief executive isn't keen on the idea. He thinks people would be bound to talk and it would be bad PR for the council if it got out in the press that there's a poison pen operating in the building. Talking of which, I take it that you saw the piece in the local rag?"

Jeremy nodded. He had. As no doubt had many other people in the town. The coroner's remarks at the inquest had been reported verbatim.

"So when will you start?" he asked.

"We're fairly quiet at the moment so probably tomorrow."

"So it's worth a try, do you think?" asked Jeremy.

"Definitely worth a try. It's a bit hit-and-miss, true, but you never know. We've got to do something. The letters seem to be coming quite frequently now and I might get lucky."

CHAPTER TWENTY-FOUR

The man switched on his laptop and then sat back while he reflected on his day. That bloody stupid police officer, did he honestly think that he didn't recognise him for what he was? He'd spotted him straight away. He might not have been in uniform, but it was obvious. If it looks like a copper and smells like a copper then it probably is a copper. And as for hanging around the pigeonholes with a screwdriver sticking out of his overall pocket and pretending to measure the skirting board, it was laughable. Anyway, as luck would have it, he hadn't been going to post anything today, he'd only gone over to the pigeonholes when he'd picked up the email telling him that his parcel had been delivered. He often gave the town hall as his delivery address. There were too many thieving bastards around to risk leaving things lying on door steps.

He flexed his fingers and wriggled his shoulders. Time to get to work. Ten minutes later he sat back and admired his latest creation. God, this stuff was addictive. This one, he thought, particularly good. It would definitely give a kick up the arse to that stupid old dodderer, Michael, who worked in the post room. The miserable sod should have been pensioned off years ago, the council only kept him on because they felt sorry for him. Well, he didn't feel sorry for him. As far as he could see the idle bastard just sat around drinking tea all day. There was virtually no post to deal with. Most people communicated via email or through the website. Hardly anybody wrote letters to the council anymore.

His only regret was that he couldn't think of a way to be around when Michael read that he'd been seen accessing extreme pornography and that the police were involved and would shortly be paying him a visit. It would be a laugh, he thought, if it was actually true and Michael really had been looking at that kind of stuff. Actually, he wouldn't be surprised if he had been. It was just the sort of thing that he would do. Everybody knew that the female staff, especially the young ones, avoided the post room like the plague. It was all very well the council proudly telling all and sundry how inclusive they were. Some people didn't deserve to be included. In fact they should be positively excluded.

He read the letter over again and then pressed print. He'd enjoyed writing that one, but what he'd really like was to get a letter to Jeremy Goodman. There was something about the man that just annoyed him. That piece in the local press about his appointment to Sir Franks, with the stupid smiling photograph of him with his wife and Carlos, made him sick. They'd written about him as though he was some sort of saint. Oh yes, Sir Franks was lucky to have got him all right. But who did they think they were kidding? Sir Franks would have been lucky to get anybody.

His mouth tightened. Goodman was just the sort of person he really detested. The sort that always got all the nice stuff in life, the sort for whom good fortune just lay in piles around his feet. He'd bet Jeremy Goodman had experienced a really comfortable, happy childhood. One in which his father dressed up as Father Christmas and took him for holidays by the sea, complete with bucket and spade, and his mother made apple pies and took him to the park to play on the swings. Jeremy Goodman hadn't had to wear second-hand school uniform or comfort his mother as she tried to help his father balance the books on the business that was crashing down around their ears. Jeremy Goodman hadn't had to watch his father literally work himself to death. And Jeremy Goodman hadn't had to witness his mother start displaying the terrifying symptoms of early onset dementia shortly after.

He let his mind run back to that dreadful day, the day of her diagnosis. It had been a rainy Wednesday afternoon and he had sat with her in the cheerless waiting room, reading the posters telling him to book his flu vaccination and to eat his five-a-day, all the time knowing in his heart what was coming. When they had finally made it into the consulting room he hadn't been at all surprised as he sat there listening to the tired looking doctor explaining to him what the future held. He'd known for some time that all was not well and at least the doctor had paid him the respect of being honest with him. There had been no attempt to dress it up or soften the blow and, on reflection, he was thankful for that. It was better to have no hope than false hope.

It had started soon after his father had died and it had been a while before it had really registered. At first it was just small things, like repeatedly asking what day it was or constantly misplacing her spectacles or book she was reading and then finding them in the fridge or cutlery drawer. Later it was the bigger things. Food that she'd cooked all her life for her husband and son suddenly became a mystery to her. He would find her in the kitchen staring at the jumble of ingredients that she'd laid out and clearly at a loss as to what to do with them. By the time she'd got to the stage of wandering the street in her nightdress looking for his father, it had been game over. And then he'd been left with the nightmare of navigating the care system. He had naively thought that it would be a simple matter of choosing a residential home for her, getting her settled in, and that the state would take care of the rest. He'd quickly discovered that the cradle-to-the-grave health care promise on which the NHS had been founded was an empty one in the twenty-first century.

Clearly his mother couldn't remain at home. What she needed was residential care with twenty-four hour supervision, but residential care had to be paid for and the cost was exorbitant. The state would only pay if the care required was what it considered to be nursing care, rather than what they called social care, and it had been made very clear to him that as far as the local authority was concerned, his mother fell into the latter category.

His father had left no money, but he had insured his life which had paid off the mortgage on the little house his parents had jointly owned. But, as he had discovered to his horror, it would have to be sold to pay for his mother's care. The only way she could keep the house was if she had what they called a qualifying dependent living there, and being neither old enough nor young enough, he didn't qualify. The other alternative was for her to remain at home with him as her full-time carer, a prospect that appalled him. When she had suddenly died, he had felt nothing but relief. It was, really, the best for all concerned.

But Jeremy Goodman wouldn't have gone through an experience like that. His parents were probably alive and still had all their marbles. They would be like those good-looking, slim retired couples on the television adverts who went on cruises together and were pictured in their leisure wear, clinking glasses and gazing adoringly into each other's eyes as the ocean rolled out behind them. Jeremy Goodman wouldn't have spent hours on the phone and in meetings with social workers trying to work out the best way forward while being blocked at every turn. Jeremy Goodman wouldn't have worried about how to pay off his father's debts or watched as his mother crumbled into a confused incontinent mess. No, it was obvious that Jeremy Goodman had truly led a charmed and sunny life. Well, a little shower of poison rain was about to drop into it. Goodman deserved a letter, but he'd make it the last one. Truth to tell, spotting that copper hanging around in the pigeonhole room had unnerved him and it was about time he wrapped it up anyway. He had other things to be getting on with.

If it was going to be the last letter it would have to be a really good one though, one that accused him of something like embezzling school funds or indulging in what was now called inappropriate behaviour, or both. Something that, if it were true, would finish his career for good and probably his marriage as well. But what if Goodman simply ignored it? He was just the sort that would. He'd report it to the police and that would be that. He felt suddenly despondent. The problem was that Goodman didn't have a vulnerability, or at least not one that he was aware of. With Miss Bateman it was obviously her disability, and the others all had their Achilles heel too. Even with Alfonso, once he'd realised how much his café meant to him, it had been all too easy. With Carlos though it had been different. He thought about him for a moment. There was no denying it, those letters had been personal.

From the first time he'd seen his attractive face and casual easy-going manner he'd hated him. It had been a visceral, choking feeling that had taken him by surprise. He'd spent considerable time looking at Carlos's social media posts, fuelling his hatred. Carlos lived with the Goodmans, he knew. There were a number of smiling pictures of the three of them, the most recent one being some kind of barbecue in what looked like their back garden. A happy family. He felt his face muscles tighten and his heart start to beat faster. The Goodmans should have left him in whatever slum he'd crawled out of. Why should Carlos have it so easy when he'd had to fight tooth and nail for everything he'd got? What had Carlos ever done to deserve it? There was no justice, no fairness. Somehow, when all this was over, he'd find a way to get at him. In the meantime there was Goodman to consider.

There was nothing about Jeremy Goodman that he could identify, nothing that would make him reluctant to show the letter to anybody else. He'd googled him, but there was nothing out of the way. No hint at any weakness, only the facts of his career. Social media hadn't yielded anything either. Then came a sudden rush of excitement. There was, he suddenly realised, an excellent way to upset him. Why not send the letter to his wife? Something really nasty that neither of them would want to reveal to the world. He could include some stuff about Carlos in it. That would really dial things up. But how would he get it to her?

He got up and walked over to the window while he thought about it. So far, he had delivered the letters personally, so to speak, but why not post one? The more he thought about it the more excited he became. It would be relatively easy to find Goodman's address, a quick check of the electoral register would do it. And if he couldn't find it there, he'd find another way. As a last resort he could follow him home, after all he knew where he worked. And then, and he had to admit this would be a real stroke of genius, he could put it through the post room at the town hall. External mail was dropped into a post sack in the pigeonhole room for franking and posting out. If he did it that way, then it might also implicate Michael.

Outside, the evening had settled in and the street lights were beginning to twinkle into life. This time of day always made him feel restless, perhaps because it reminded him of his mother. It had been at this time of day that she had died.

CHAPTER TWENTY-FIVE

Aubrey lay stretched along the arm of the sofa and watched as Molly flicked through a magazine, turning the pages and barely glancing at the content. She clearly wasn't reading it. She seemed, he thought, distracted. As though she had something on her mind. She hadn't even told him and Vincent off when she'd discovered them on a work surface in the utility room trying to open the cat treats. She had simply scooped them up and turfed them off. Normally they would have been chucked out for that kind of behaviour, but not today.

Molly put her magazine down and looked up at the sound of a key in the front door.

"Carlos, you're home late. Was the traffic bad?"

Carlos flopped down on the sofa and ran his hand along Aubrey's back.

"No, not really. It was busy at work today, like, more than usual. It's been raining so loads of people came in for lunch and tea. And Jamal's off sick."

"What's the matter with him."

Carlos looked up from stroking Aubrey and shrugged.

"Dunno. Some bug or other. Molly, are you all right? You look a bit pale."

"I'm fine."

"You don't look fine. Do you want a cup of tea or anything?"

"I told you, I'm fine."

Carlos and Aubrey looked at her in alarm. Molly never spoke sharply. Well, hardly ever, thought Aubrey. Only when she was really cross about something and even then it didn't last. She said what she had to say and that would be the end of it. He climbed off the arm of the sofa and jumped onto her lap. In spite of what she claimed, she clearly wasn't fine and the least he could do was his cat duty of offering a bit of comfort. She reached down and rested her hand on his head.

"I'm sorry, Carlos. I didn't mean to snap."

"What is it, Molly? Has something happened? Has somebody upset you?"

She frowned.

"No. I'm just a bit tired that's all."

She picked up her magazine again but then threw it down at the sound of a car outside. Lifting Aubrey to the floor, she jumped to her feet and ran out to meet Jeremy.

Carlos and Aubrey stared at each other. They all loved Jeremy, but they didn't usually feel the need to run to greet him when he returned home. They listened to the sound of a low murmur of voices in the hall. Whatever Molly was telling him, it clearly wasn't for their ears. Carlos leaned over towards Aubrey.

"Something's going on," he whispered.

He sat back again, his expression strained. Aubrey knew what he was thinking. Change for Carlos usually meant something bad, just as it did for the cats. In all of their short lives, it had been their experience that anything out of the ordinary was hardly ever for the good. He crept across the room and parked himself on Carlos's lap. Whatever it was, they might as well face it together.

"What do you think it is?" Carlos kept his voice low. "Do you think, like, someone's died or something?"

Aubrey thought about it for a moment. It was possible, he supposed, but he doubted it. When somebody died, people were usually nicer to each other, they didn't get all irritable. He flinched as the sound of Jeremy's voice was suddenly raised and the door was flung open. Without glancing at either Carlos or Aubrey, he strode through to the kitchen and slammed the door behind him. Molly rushed after him, her head down and what were unmistakeable streaks of tears on her cheeks. Aubrey winced as Carlos clutched at him, his long slim fingers digging into his fur.

"I'm telling you, Moll, I will not have it." Jeremy's voice exploded into rage and crashed through the wall. Aubrey watched in alarm as Carlos's bottom lip began to tremble slightly. They didn't need to strain to hear what was being said now.

"This has got to stop. I'll kill him. How dare he? How *dare* he?"

Carlos took a sharp breath.

"He's shouting," he muttered. "He never shouts."

He does actually, thought Aubrey. Only not when you're around and usually as the result of some provocation, like that time he hit his thumb with a lump hammer. The air had been pretty blue that day.

The door suddenly opened again and Jeremy marched in. Making straight for the small cabinet in the corner, he yanked the door open and pulled out a bottle of whisky. He turned and looked at Carlos and Aubrey cowering on the sofa. They stared back at him, their eyes wide. He smiled suddenly and lowered his shoulders.

"All right, you two, stop looking like the mad axeman has just broken in." He shrugged off his suit jacket and draped it across the back of the sofa. Loosening his tie, he called through to the kitchen. "Moll, come on in here. Let's talk about this together."

Molly, pale but not crying now, came slowly through from the kitchen and settled herself back in the arm chair. Jeremy sat down on the chair opposite and, reaching over, patted her hand.

"It's okay, Moll. I think we'd better tell them."

Aubrey gave a small grunt of satisfaction. He loved it that Jeremy always included him in everything. The other night he'd even asked him if he was enjoying a film that they were watching. He hadn't actually been particularly watching it, being far more interested in a large spider that was inching its way towards the door, but it was nice to be asked. He settled back against Carlos as Jeremy turned to face them.

"Moll has received one of the poison pen letters. It came in the post today."

"What did it say?" asked Carlos.

Jeremy looked at Molly who gave a slight almost imperceptible shake of the head.

"I think it's better if you don't see it, Carlos. Not yet, at least. The thing about it is that the envelope was franked at the town hall, which really just confirms what we were fairly sure of anyway."

"What are we going to do?" Carlos trickled his hand across Aubrey's head, a soothing gesture that comforted both of them. "I mean, like, what's Molly ever done to anyone?"

"What have any of you done?" said Jeremy.

He sat down and ran his hand through his hair.

"Let's think about this logically," he continued. "Whoever sent the letter to Molly clearly knows who she is and where she lives. It can't just be a random coincidence. So, why Molly?"

Carlos turned to Molly.

"Do you know anyone who works at the town hall?"

Molly shook her head.

"I don't think so. Nobody that I'm aware of, anyway."

"But somebody knows you," he said.

"Or," Jeremy suddenly sat up straighter. "Somebody knows who she is."

Carlos frowned.

"What?"

"Somebody knows who she is," he repeated. "What if the letter wasn't sent to upset Molly but to upset somebody else?"

"You mean..." Carlos hesitated.

"What if the letter was sent to upset me. Or you," Jeremy added.

Molly shot him a warning glance.

"Anyway," he spoke more slowly now, his tone thoughtful. "Whatever the intention, whoever is writing this filth is spreading the net and God knows how much more damage he'll do before he's stopped."

"It might be a she," said Molly.

Jeremy gave a short humourless laugh.

"Not with language like that."

Molly smiled. "You'd be surprised."

Jeremy reached across to his jacket and pulled out a small notebook with a pen attached. Since he'd taken up the headship of Sir Franks he carried it with him always. Old-fashioned pen and paper was still the best way to make an instant note of anything that he wanted to remember later, and he checked it at the end of every day. Flicking the notebook open to a fresh page he wrote the date at the top.

"So, what do we actually know? Or think we know," he added.

"He works at the town hall," said Carlos.

"And he uses Alfonso's café," added Molly.

"And he takes risks," suggested Carlos.

Jeremy nodded approvingly at Carlos. "Very good."

Molly and Carlos watched as he scribbled on the notepad.

"Anything else?" he asked.

Molly shook her head.

"Not really. I mean at one time we could have said that it's someone who can use a computer, but that's just about everybody now."

She sat back and thought for a moment.

"Remember that we did think that perhaps, maybe, Jamal..." she hesitated and looked at Carlos. "Because of him being near the pigeonholes that time."

"He knows Alfonso, too," said Jeremy. "He helped him with the catering after Rissa's funeral. I saw him there. How has he been at work, Carlos? I mean, does he seem different in any way?"

Carlos shrugged. "I don't think so. But he's been off sick a bit lately so we haven't seen so much of him."

"I'm going to put him on the list," said Jeremy. "Don't worry, Carlos. This is just between us for the moment."

"Can you think of anybody else?" asked Molly.

"Well," Jeremy hesitated. He had felt slightly ashamed of himself for suspecting Gerald Crawley. After all, just because he personally disliked the man it didn't make him a criminal. But then again...

"There's one of the governors." He spoke slowly. "Gerald Crawley. I think I've mentioned him to you before Molly."

Molly nodded. "The one that never stops talking?"

"Yes, him. I'm probably being unfair, but there's just something about him, and he fits the criteria. He works at the town hall, so he might easily visit Alfonso's. And he knew Rissa.

At least, he knew that she'd been appointed. Also, he knows that I'm married."

"How would he know where you lived though?" asked Carlos.

"It wouldn't take too much to find out. I'm going to put him on the list. For now, anyway."

Carlos leaned forward and pinned his elbows to his knees.

"The thing is, Jeremy, that's only two people. It still leaves, like, hundreds of other people that it could be."

Jeremy flipped the notebook shut and threw it to one side. He sighed.

"I know. You're absolutely right. But it's just so frustrating. This bastard is going around causing untold damage and nothing seems to stop him."

CHAPTER TWENTY-SIX

Carlos couldn't remember the last time he had felt so, well, just so happy. In fact, he thought that it was the happiest he had ever been. In his whole life. Even better than when his mother had given him the toy fire engine he'd longed for on his fourth birthday. All right, the memory was slightly ruined later by his father throwing it out of the apartment window in a drunken rage, but what he remembered best was that perfect moment. The sheer joy of pulling off the wrapping paper to discover the gleaming red truck. It was based on a British model and had everything, even an extending ladder and a little hose that could be pulled out. Where his mother had got the money from he had no idea and at four years old he hadn't asked. But that fire engine had been his heart's desire, the best thing that he could remember. Until now.

He and Teddy couldn't have picked a better day. Everything had gone completely to plan. Even the trains had been running on time. The rain that had fallen with a steady patter over the last few days had ceased and bright autumn sunshine had broken through. They had made the most of it. There was hardly an inch of the city centre that they hadn't explored. To him, the best thing was the number of small bistros and cafés and he'd pinned his nose to their glass windows and studied their menus with a keen professional eye. In culinary terms, Brighton looked like where it was at. He'd definitely put it on his list of possible venues for when he had his own restaurant. He raised his glass and grinned. Buying Teddy a cocktail before they had to get their trains home was the perfect ending to a brilliant day.

She looked across at him, her face suddenly serious.

"Carlos, you haven't said anything today about those letters. Have they stopped now?"

He shook his head. "I don't know. I don't think so."

He hadn't mentioned them, he knew, because he hadn't wanted anything to spoil their time together. He'd wanted to keep every moment free from the taint of everyday life. He looked at Teddy's lovely face. It didn't matter. They'd had a perfect day and even the poison pen couldn't take that away from them.

"I've been thinking about them." Teddy fell silent for a moment and then continued, speaking slowly. "The letter that went to Molly."

"What about it?"

"You don't know what it said?"

"No. They wouldn't show it to me. It must have been pretty bad though, Molly was crying."

Teddy thought for a moment.

"What if there's something else behind all this? Something that's not just about being nasty? Something that nobody's thought of?"

"Like what?"

"I don't know. But after you told me about it, I googled poison pen letters."

Carlos leaned forward, interested.

"What did you find out?"

"Well, first it's more common than you might think. From the stories that I read, the main reason for it seems to be either jealousy or some kind of hatred. Or sometimes a sort of power grab."

"What does that mean?"

"Well, if you make someone scared of you it makes you feel powerful. Like the Nazis," she added.

Carlos thought about what Teddy had just said. It was true. The biggest bully in his school year at Sir Franks hadn't been a Nazi, at least he didn't he think was, but he had strutted around as though he owned the place. Until one of the girls had chucked a big stone at his head and he'd started crying. If he was honest though, a part of him had felt sorry for the boy. His instinct had told him that the boy hadn't been born a bully, something or someone had made him like that.

"What kind of people write them?" he asked.

"Years ago, it seems that it used to be mostly women. There was a famous case not far from here, they've made a film about it."

Carlos raised his eyebrows.

"Why women?"

"I think in the old days it was because they felt that they weren't allowed to lead the lives that they wanted to live, that they were stopped from doing things, and so they sort of took it out on other people. It was different for women back then. Like, did you know that if you were a teacher and you got married you had to resign? And it was ages before women were allowed to vote or anything."

"But," Carlos pointed out. "We're not in the old days now. I mean, like, women can do anything they want these days."

Teddy smiled.

"Well, not quite, but I know what you mean. That's what makes your letters interesting."

"Does it?"

"Yes. Think about it. If you were writing poison pen letters because you were angry or jealous or something, you'd write them to people that you thought had something that you wanted but couldn't have. If you see what I mean."

Carlos nodded. He did see what she meant.

"So if you were poor, you'd write them to rich people," he said. "Or people that you thought were rich. Like, people that live in big houses and that."

"Yes, exactly," Teddy continued. "Or if you were a teenager you might write one to someone who's really popular or good at sport or something."

Carlos frowned slightly as he thought about it.

"Do you think it's possible that it might be a teenager?"

Teddy shook her head.

"No, not really. I think that a teenager would be more likely to write poison pen stuff to another teenager, not to people who are old enough to be their mum and dad. Okay, I know that you and those girls are young, but the man that owns the café and that disabled lady that you told me about isn't, and neither is Molly. I mean," she conceded, "she's not old, but she's not a teenager. Also, it's the way that the letters are written."

"What do you mean?"

"I think a younger person would be more likely to use texting or email."

"But then the person who got the message would know who it's from."

"Not necessarily. Someone could just buy a pay-as-you-go phone. And it's easy to just create an email address, Casper does it all the time."

At the mention of Casper, Carlos couldn't help but smile.

Teddy's younger brother was the scourge of every teacher that had ever had the misfortune to encounter him, but there was no denying that as well as being a cheerful and exuberant soul he had an extremely creative brain.

"How's the Casper Beaumont International Detective Agency going?" he asked.

Teddy groaned.

"Don't ask. Dad found out about it and he's put a padlock on the summer house door. Anyway," she continued, "my point is that if it was a young person writing poison pen stuff, it would be something instant. They wouldn't put it on paper, and they definitely wouldn't post anything. Like, through a letter box or in a pigeonhole. To be honest, I didn't even know what a pigeonhole was until you told me. So I reckon it must be, well, not necessarily an old person, but not a young one."

It was true about writing letters, thought Carlos. It was definitely what older people did. He'd received letters, like when he got his driving licence and his exam certificates and stuff like that, but he didn't think he'd ever written one, not an actual letter, on paper. He and Teddy had once talked about doing it but in the end they hadn't. So Teddy was almost certainly right. The poison pen probably wasn't a young person.

"Let's look at the facts," said Teddy. "Let's see if there's some sort of connection between the people who've received the letters. We need to think about how the poison pen is selecting who to write to. What was so special about them that they got picked out?"

Carlos shrugged.

"No idea. Maybe it was just random."

"No, I don't think so," said Teddy. "Hardly anything is just random. There must be something, even if it's just, say, alphabetical or you all belong to the same club or something. Let's think about it logically."

"Right. But don't forget, there might be some people who haven't come forward. Some people that we don't know about."

"True. All right, so of those that we do know about, let's ask ourselves, who are they?"

"Well, me and Molly to start with, we've both had letters. I've had two," said Carlos. "And Alfonso, the bloke that owns the café in town, he's had a couple. Then there's the girls that work at the town hall. I don't know how many they've had." He thought for a moment. "And Miss Bates. And then there was that teacher that died. Clarissa Ingram.

Teddy took a sip of her drink and sat back.

"Okay, tell me what you know about them."

Carlos thought for a moment.

"I never met that teacher but Jeremy liked her. He said that she was really good with the kids. And I know Alfonso because I've been in his café. He seems like a nice bloke, sort of cheerful and that. He's always smiling anyway. I think he lives on his own. He's got a cat," he added. "Called Muriel."

"What about the others?"

"I know Chloe Kennedy, because she comes into the staff restaurant sometimes and I recognise her a bit. She used to go to Sir Franks. She was in the year below me. I think her family's a bit dodgy."

Teddy looked interested, momentarily distracted.

"Dodgy in what way?"

"Well, I think her mum and dad drink."

Teddy laughed.

"My mum and dad drink, too."

"But they don't go rolling round the town picking fights with people."

"True," Teddy conceded. "So what have all the recipients of the letters got in common?"

Carlos shrugged, his face perplexed.

"Nothing. I mean, like we're all human but that's about it. We're not the same ages or anything. I was going to say that we all work at the town hall, but Molly and Alfonso don't. That teacher didn't either. So no, nothing."

"Exactly. I mean," Teddy leaned forward, her pretty face animated. "It's not like you're all rich, or all famous or anything. There's nothing that connects you. You don't even all know each other. So what other reason could there be?"

CHAPTER TWENTY-SEVEN

Carlos stared through the window as the train pulled out of the station. Only two more stops and he'd be home. The evening was closing in now and his reflection stared back at him. From his pocket the sweet strains of Pachelbel's Canon filtered out. Teddy had chosen it as his ring tone. He'd never heard it before, but now he loved it. Apart from anything else, every time his phone rang it made him think of her.

"Did you get your train all right?"

Even though he'd seen her less than an hour ago, his heart turned slightly at the sound of her voice.

"Yeah, I'm on it now. I had a great time today, did you?"

He strained to hear her response as the train entered a tunnel. It was no good. The connection had gone dead. Never mind, he'd ring her when he got home. He switched screen and turned to his photographs. Teddy had looked so pretty when he'd waved her off that he hadn't been able to resist taking a picture.

He stared down at the image. He'd been worried when she'd first gone to university – worried that she would meet someone else, that once she was surrounded by clever, interesting, posh boys she would find him dull and boring by comparison. But, so far, nothing seemed to have changed between them. They spoke on most days, usually via WhatsApp, and meeting in Brighton had been her idea. Anyway, university wasn't forever and the terms seemed pretty short. By the time she graduated, he would have enough experience to think about starting up a place of his own.

At the thought of his restaurant his heart lifted. He just knew he could make it work. He'd keep it small to begin with, maybe one of those pop-up things, with just a few dishes on the menu. But those few dishes would be made with the best ingredients and cooked to absolute perfection. There would be no shortcuts. Everything would be sourced locally and freshly made on the premises. He would receive fantastic reviews and then he'd buy somewhere bigger and be even more successful and famous people would start coming in and it would be, like, one of those places where you had to book months in advance to get a table. Or maybe he wouldn't even have a booking system. He'd just let people in so that everybody had a chance. Then he'd write cookery books and people would bring them to him to sign. Everything would be just brilliant, and there to share it all with him would be Teddy... he jumped as the announcement came over the speaker. Due to an incident on the line, all passengers were requested to leave at the next stop. Pulling his jacket back on he made his way towards the doors.

The early evening crowd jostled uncomfortably on the platform. Clearly the train on which Carlos had been travelling wasn't the only one to be cancelled partway through the journey. He pulled out his phone again and, head down, began scrolling through his messages and email. Nothing in particular, only a note from his old college friend, Rubble, so called because his real name was Barney, recounting his latest misadventure.

Employed by his ever-patient father at his hotel, Rubble's

title was trainee manager. Whether Rubble would ever complete his training to a level that earned him the full title of manager was a moot point. Rubble, as happy as the day was long, didn't seem to mind one way or the other. Carlos smiled to himself at the memory of one of their lecturers saying that Rubble couldn't run a whelk stall. He wasn't sure what a whelk stall was, but whatever it was he was pretty certain that the lecturer hadn't been wrong. And then he felt it. A pair of hands. A strong shove to the small of his back, and he tumbled forward onto the track.

Molly looked across at Jeremy.

"He should be home by now. He said that he'd be back by eight and it's nearly ten o'clock."

Jeremy pulled his eyes away from the television screen.

"He's probably just lost track of time. Or his train's been delayed or something. Give him a call."

"I've tried. He's not answering his phone."

"Perhaps he's just busy or he hasn't heard it or something."

Even as he spoke, Jeremy realised what an unlikely scenario that was. Carlos's phone was as much a part of him as his arms and legs, it was never out of earshot. And he would never ignore a call from either him or Molly.

"What do you suggest?" he asked. "I mean, he is eighteen now. If he chooses to come home late then that's up to him. Look, let's give it another half an hour before we start worrying."

Molly opened her mouth to speak and then closed it again at the sound of a car door slamming outside. They watched in silence as Carlos entered the room. A small dressing was taped just above his right eye and a large purple bruise shadowed across his right cheek. He sat down and stared back at them for a moment, his dark eyes sombre.

"Sorry I'm late," he said at last.

Molly swallowed in an effort to compose herself before speaking.

"What happened? Are you all right?" she asked.

Carlos nodded. "I'm okay."

"You don't look okay."

Jeremy leaned towards him, his face worried. Teenaged boys were particularly vulnerable to random violence, he knew. Sometimes just walking down the high street on a Friday or Saturday night and glancing at someone could end in an unwanted brawl. Carlos wouldn't be the first lad to be set on in an unprovoked attack.

"Did somebody do this to you?" he asked.

"No." Carlos paused for a moment. "I had an accident. And I've lost my phone. I've been at the hospital." He stared down at the floor. "And then I got a taxi home."

Jeremy looked across at Molly who had half-risen from her chair, and swiftly raised a finger to his lips. She sat back again.

"What sort of accident?" asked Jeremy, his tone gentle. "Did you fall over or something?"

Carlos looked up.

"Sort of," he said. He closed his eyes for a moment and took a breath before continuing. "I fell on the train track. We had to change trains and there were loads of people on the platform and I fell. Some people helped me up and my head was bleeding, so somebody called for some station first aiders."

"Oh my God." Molly's hand flew to her mouth. "You could have been killed."

"Not all the rails are live. Somebody told me afterwards. They said I'd been lucky that there hadn't been a train coming."

For several seconds none of them said anything. The

appalling mental image that Carlos's words had just conjured up had momentarily silenced all three of them.

"So what happened?" said Jeremy at last. "Did you just lose your balance?"

"I guess so. It all happened really quickly. Some trains had been cancelled and the platform was really crowded. I was just standing there and then..."

Molly stood up, her face white.

"I think we all need a drink."

Jeremy tipped his head to one side and looked at his foster son.

"What is it that you're not telling us, Carlos?"

Carlos took a sip from the whisky that Molly passed him.

"Nothing."

Jeremy waited.

"Well..."

"Go on."

"I think somebody pushed me. On purpose, I mean."

Jeremy stared at him.

"Are you sure?"

Carlos nodded.

"I think so. I felt it. I was near the edge of the platform. I wasn't to start with but then more and more people were coming onto it and I sort of got pushed to the front. I was just checking my phone and then I felt it."

"You don't think that somebody just bumped into you? I mean, you said yourself that it was very crowded."

Carlos shook his head.

"No. It was two hands. Definitely. Like this."

He put his glass down and holding his hands up palm outwards he made a shoving motion.

"So you think it was deliberate?" asked Jeremy.

"Yes. I think it must have been. It was probably, like, some sort of random mad person."

Jeremy had been about to say that they ought to call the police but, although Carlos looked better than he had when he first came in, he probably wasn't up to making a statement tonight. Instead he said, "What happened after you fell? Can you remember?"

"I've tried, but it's all sort of a bit blurred. It happened really quickly. I was reading a message from Rubble and then the next thing I remember is hitting my head. I couldn't work out what had happened at first and I sort of looked up and I could see all these arms reaching down and people trying to pull me back up onto the platform. Then these first aid people came and they said that I ought to go to hospital. Because I was bleeding and because of the shock and that. So one of them called an ambulance. Then when I got there I had to wait ages in A&E before anybody could see me. It was when I was at the hospital that I realised that I didn't have my phone. Otherwise I would have rung you."

Jeremy looked at him. He had been about to say that Carlos could probably have borrowed someone else's phone just to make a quick call to him or Molly. But then he realised that Carlos almost certainly didn't keep any numbers in his head. Any more than he did. In his childhood there had been one telephone which was a landline and it was kept in the hall on a little table called the telephone table. He had known the number of that telephone by heart, as he had known all his landline numbers, and could even recite them to this day. But when it came to mobiles he didn't have a clue. He didn't even know his own number. He didn't need to. Every number he needed was stored in the mobile's memory. Which was great. Fine. Except when you lost your phone.

"Come on, I'll make you some cheese on toast. With double

ketchup," he said, rising to his feet. "And then I think you ought to be in bed. We can talk about all this a bit more in the morning."

As he walked through to the kitchen, he shivered slightly as a new thought struck him. What if Carlos hadn't been pushed by some random mad person as he called it? What if it hadn't been pure chance? It was a thought that threw a whole new chilling light on the incident.

CHAPTER TWENTY-EIGHT

He opened his eyes and stared straight ahead of him. He was in his bedroom, but he might as well have been on a distant planet, somewhere far away across the galaxy where even the stars were dark. He felt nothing but emptiness. He wouldn't sleep now, he knew. He was lucky really to have slept at all. The fog of despair had descended on him several hours ago, as he knew that it would. He had felt it coming, creeping slowly along behind him, reaching out its damp little tentacles, looking for a way in. It was nothing new. He was used to it. He couldn't even remember when it had first started. Probably when he was a teenager, perhaps before. Nothing had been done about it. He couldn't remember now if he had even told his parents. In a strange way, it had seemed natural that he should be depressed. They all were, they had something to be depressed about. Somebody had once said to him that money didn't make you happy. Well, it would have made them happy. They would have been able to turn the heating on for a start.

Once the depression settled in and spread its elbows nothing could shift it but time itself. He knew that, and he accepted it. He would just have to wait it out, as he always did.

Sometimes it threatened, like a gathering storm, and then just evaporated like a passing cloud. Other times it lay in wait, patiently searching for a crack to appear in his defences, like a malevolent sniper lining up the crosshairs from a rooftop. He knew when the crack had appeared this time. It had been unexpectedly seeing the boy.

He'd spotted Carlos on the train straight away. Those distinctive good looks were hard to miss. Moving seat so that he could see Carlos more clearly but not be seen himself, he had got up when the boy had and followed him onto the platform. It had been easy to shuffle forward and move in close behind him. Normally people kept their distance at stations but last night there had been no choice. They were rammed in together like the proverbial sardines and with each new wave of people that came onto the platform they were all pushed forward.

Several times the announcement had been made that, for their own safety, people should move away from the edge. Of course, in true British fashion, nobody had complied. If anything they had moved even closer, determined to get on the next train that came in. For several minutes he had stood right behind him, he could smell the freshness of the boy's skin and the thickness of his dark hair had almost tickled his nose. The bile within him had risen.

In the chaos that had followed Carlos falling onto the track with people shouting and running, it had been easy to melt away again towards the back of the crowd. But not before he had covertly kicked away the mobile that had dropped from Carlos's hand as he fell. He had picked it up and slipped it into his pocket and then, looking neither right nor left, he had left the station and walked quietly towards the taxi rank.

As he waited for his taxi, he risked a quick glance back. The other passengers had managed to haul Carlos to safety and had cleared a ring around him. Disappointing in some respects, nevertheless it was probably just as well. His future plans didn't include being banged up on a murder charge, even though he thought it unlikely that any cameras at the station had captured what he'd done. Everybody was jammed in so tightly that the quick movement of his hands wouldn't have been picked up. Neither would it have been remarkable that he had left the station. By that point, a number of people had given up and were looking for alternative ways to finish their journeys.

When he reached home, he had sprawled out on the sofa and cradled a large glass of wine while he thought about Carlos. His overwhelming emotion had been that of resentment. Earlier in the day, he had been feeling quite happy – for once content with his lot. He'd got lots of things done that he'd needed to do, ticking them off the list, and then he had met Jeannie at a small hotel that they sometimes used and which wasn't too particular about guests that only wanted a room for an hour or two. There was something about the seediness of the hotel that he liked, it added to the illicit thrill. He'd taken a couple of bottles of wine with him, as he usually did, and she had told him about the flat which she owned with her husband which was standing empty while it was being redecorated between tenants. The management of it was left to her so she had given him a key, which he'd been pleased about. Situated on the other side of the park, the flat was in a pleasant area. It was the kind of area that he might like to live in himself one day. All had been well in his world.

Any qualms that he had experienced last week about telling Jeannie what he had been doing had vanished. He'd needed to tell someone how clever he was, he had needed that undisguised admiration, and she had given it. She hadn't been shocked, as he had known she wouldn't be. Her knowing had brought them closer together and they had talked about the future, a future in which they would have everything that they wanted.

He'd already decided that the letter to Goodman's wife would be the last, and he had no doubt that with the passage of time the police would lose interest. Other priorities would emerge and it would remain as just another unsolved case. Nobody would care anymore, especially after it stopped. All in all, everything had been going along very nicely. And then he'd seen Carlos. Lounging in his seat with his long legs stretched before him, with all the assured careless insouciance of youth. He had felt the bitterness well up again.

He thought again about the feeling as he had shoved both his hands with all the force he could muster right into the small of Carlos's back. It had felt good. No, it had felt more than good. It had felt terrific. He hadn't planned it. When he had crept up behind him on the platform, he hadn't had any particular idea in mind, other than to perhaps aim a swift spiteful kick at the back of his leg. But standing there, so close to him, it had been as if his hands had moved of their own volition. In the split second that followed, his instinct for survival had kicked in and he had swiftly put distance between them. Would he do it again if he got the chance? Probably not. It had been a risk too far, and he knew it. He was fairly certain that he'd got away with it this time, but he couldn't depend on being lucky again. Luck was what losers relied on and, whatever else he was, he wasn't a loser.

He sighed and swung his legs out of bed. He glanced at the bedside clock. It was not quite five o'clock. The worst time to be up and around. Too early to do anything. Too late to catch up with any proper sleep. He made his way downstairs and sat down at the kitchen table. The phone that he'd picked up was lying there. He stared down at the screen. It had cracked as it had hit the hard concrete of the platform, a thin sliver across the top right-hand corner.

That there had been several missed calls, he knew. He had

heard it ringing on his way home and even the ring tone had annoyed him. Some pathetic classical music. It just would be. Carlos couldn't have some stupid pop song like all the other teenagers. He had to have something pretentious. It had probably been chosen for him by Goodman. But at least it had reminded him to switch the thing off. The last thing he wanted was for it to be tracked to his house. He wasn't sure what he was going to do with it yet, if anything, but there was a certain satisfaction in knowing that Carlos would be not just inconvenienced by its loss but probably devastated.

At work the other month some stupid woman thought she had lost her phone. She had been practically hysterical, squawking and flapping about all over the place. Until she remembered that she'd left it in her coat pocket. But there was no doubting that, these days, the loss of a mobile phone was, to many people, nothing short of catastrophic.

He picked the phone up and flipped it between his hands. It was quite likely that it was low on charge now, if not already dead. It didn't matter, it was going in the bin anyway. He ran his fingers over the cracked screen. What little power houses mobile phones were. Unlike the early house-brick mobiles on which you could make and receive calls and not much else, most modern mobiles could tell you all sorts of things about a person. People didn't just use their phones to talk to each other. They played games on them, they read books, they searched the internet. They took photographs, they made videos. They even paid for goods and services with them. He smiled to himself. He had a vague memory of seeing some footage of a black and white advertisement on one of his favourite nostalgia television shows. Something about never being alone with some brand of cigarette and there had been a picture of a man with a hat looking like Frank Sinatra. These days you could write that about mobiles. You were never alone with a mobile phone.

He felt a sudden surge of excitement, the earlier cloud of depression lifting and floating away. Of course. It was obvious. Inside that phone were all Carlos's contacts. Not only his contacts but his photographs and emails. His texts. Everything. Wide awake now, he turned over the possibilities. Picking up the phone had been even more of a bonus than he'd first thought. It was obviously locked but that wasn't a problem. There was a guy who ran a stall in the market. He sold all sorts of chargers, and for the right price he'd unlock any phone.

CHAPTER TWENTY-NINE

Aubrey, Vincent and Moses trailed slowly across the park. While none of them quite acknowledged it, they were bored. Well, Moses wasn't. He was content just to be with his friends, but Aubrey and Vincent were definitely feeling a twinge of ennui. It wasn't so much that they were dissatisfied, more that they weren't satisfied. They'd called round on Muriel, but she'd been out doing some Muriel thing and Alfonso had been too busy opening up the café to pay them much attention, so they'd taken themselves off again. It had been Vincent's idea to take a stroll in the park. The fine weather of the last few days had held and it would, he said, do them all good to get out in the fresh air. They could have a go on the swings if there was nobody around.

Aubrey watched as Moses suddenly rolled onto his back and waved his little legs in the air. That cat, he thought, had the greatest capacity for just being happy that he had ever known. He glanced over towards the swings where a woman was supervising two small children, gently pushing them to and fro. That was the swings off then, he thought. While the woman looked okay, you could never tell. She might be one of the lunatic brigade who would start getting all red in the face and shouting at the sight of three cats advancing towards her.

He turned to Vincent.

"Now what?"

Moses rolled back onto his front and sat up.

"We could go to where I used to live."

Aubrey and Vincent looked at him in astonishment. As far as they knew, Moses had been abandoned when he wasn't much more than a kitten, and after a short spell in a rescue centre, he had lived with his owners in the same house ever since. Aubrey wasn't sure what surprised him more, the fact that Moses had ever lived anywhere else or the fact that he remembered it.

For Moses, each day was sufficient unto itself and what happened yesterday or what might happen tomorrow was as remote as the far side of the universe. Perhaps it was the rescue centre he'd been taken to that Moses was remembering. It was the kind of experience that would stick in the minds of most cats, even Moses. But Aubrey wasn't aware of any rescue centres over on this side of town.

An unpleasant thought suddenly nudged against his brain. Moses wasn't losing it, was he? There had been a cat at the last place they had lived, a dear old thing called Clara. She had definitely been a whisker short of a full set, but she had been getting on a bit. In fact, she had been ancient. You could tell just by looking at her. She'd had that cloudy-eyed look and frail little body that overtakes elderly cats. How old was Moses, he wondered.

He regarded his friend solemnly. Moses didn't look old. In fact he looked positively youthful. But then when you didn't have one brain cell to crash against another perhaps you didn't age at the same rate. Life just didn't take the same toll on you.

"Where was that then, Moses?" he asked gently. "Where was it that you used to live?"

Moses beamed at him and sprang lightly in the air.

"Come on, I'll show you."

With Moses leading the way, Aubrey and Vincent followed him through the shrubbery and across the miniature golf course. Aubrey slid a glance at Vincent.

"Do you think he knows where he's going?"

Vincent shrugged.

"I doubt it. He's probably got it all mixed up with something else. Like that time he thought he'd been away somewhere."

Aubrey smiled. That had been last summer when the children's railway had been running in the park and they'd managed to sneak a ride. For days afterwards, Moses had been convinced that they had all been on holiday.

"But it doesn't matter," Vincent continued. "It's not like we're doing anything else."

On the whole, Aubrey agreed. It was something to do, anyway. And as long as they kept Moses in sight, they could always guide him back if he accidentally strayed into dangerous territory.

They pulled up behind him as they reached the southernmost edge of the park.

"Now where?" asked Aubrey.

"Over there," said Moses.

They looked in the direction to which he was nodding. A small cul-de-sac of big Victorian houses, mostly divided into flats, lay before them. Aubrey turned to Moses.

"Did you really live here, Moses?"

Moses nodded, his eyes shining.

"With the fish."

"You lived with some fish?" asked Vincent. He looked at Aubrey who shrugged. "So how did you come to be found in the canal in that bag?"

Moses fell silent for a moment.

"I don't know."

And he probably didn't, thought Aubrey. Given that he had difficulty remembering what happened yesterday, the effort of straining to recall the events of several years ago was obviously too much for him. He looked at his little friend. His normally open expression had suddenly changed, as though a shadow had been cast across it. Perhaps he did remember what had happened, he thought. And perhaps he wished that he didn't. Nearly all of them in the cat community had things that they didn't want to talk about, some of those things being more traumatic than others. There could have been any number of reasons why Moses had been cast off by his first owners, and none of them would have been good ones.

"Come on," said Moses. "It's got a garden and everything. A nice one," he added.

They followed the little cat out of the park and along the quiet street towards the house that sat in the middle. The area had the peaceful tranquillity of one where the residents were all out at work, and it was empty of cars except for a small white van. For several moments the three of them sat on the pavement and stared up at the windows.

"Right then," said Vincent, rising to his feet. "Let's have a look at this garden."

They sidled round the side of the house and slipped easily under the garden gate. Moses was right, thought Aubrey approvingly. It was a nice garden. A very nice garden. Filled with shrubs and flowers, it was just sufficiently overgrown to provide cover. Best of all, there was a large fish pond in the middle. Instinctively the three of them edged towards it and peered in. There, among the lily pads and reeds, swam several plump goldfish. They watched in silence as the fish swam lazily in and out of the plants, unaware of the three sets of eyes fixed firmly on them. Today was turning out better than he'd hoped.

He turned to Moses.

"Can we get in?" he asked, nodding towards the house as he spoke. Much as he was enjoying watching the fish, there was still more exploring to do. And it wasn't like the fish were going anywhere.

Moses stared at the ground and thought for a moment.

"I'm not sure," he said eventually.

"Only one way to find out," said Vincent.

They followed him as he began circling round the back of the house. They paused for a moment and regarded the big plastic bins neatly stacked against one wall. Tempting, thought Aubrey, but, like the fish, the bins weren't going anywhere. Good to know that they were there though. There was nothing quite like a good bin scavenge to make you feel that the day hadn't been entirely wasted.

He jumped suddenly as the back door was yanked open and a large man, his hair pulled back neatly in a ponytail, threw a big plastic bag out onto the lawn.

"Leave the window open, Liam," he called over his shoulder. "Place could do with an airing."

A voice from inside mumbled something that the cats couldn't hear.

"No, it'll be fine, we won't be long," said the man. "There's nothing in there to nick anyway. Come on, I'll treat you to a meal deal."

The cats watched as the man let himself out of the side gate, followed shortly after by a tall, thin youth dressed in overalls that were several sizes too large for him.

"Looks like our lucky day," said Vincent, as he sprang up to the kitchen window that had been left open.

The three cats sat on the draining board and looked around them. It was a small room, just large enough to contain all the necessary equipment, and gave onto what looked like a sitting room. They jumped down and strolled through. Whatever furniture was in there was covered by big cotton sheets and several cans of paint stood on the windowsill. In the centre stood a large, paint-spattered ladder with a huge radio parked on the top rung. Aubrey turned to Moses.

"You're very quiet, Moses. Everything all right?"

Moses nodded.

"Sort of."

Aubrey looked at him, concerned. While a short time earlier he had been thinking how Moses had a seemingly endless capacity to just be happy, now the little cat looked as though he'd been told he was going to the vets. He moved closer to him.

"What is it?"

Moses looked up at him, his face glum.

"I always wanted to see this place again. I forgot where it was until today. It was when we were in the park. Then I remembered."

"Have you remembered something else, Moses?" asked Vincent.

Moses nodded.

"When I lived here it was with these two men. They were called David and Stewart, they were really kind. David used to cook me special things to eat and I had a red bowl and a red collar with our address on it. And a basket to sleep in as well, with lots of cushions. They picked me," he added, his expression suddenly brighter. "There were lots to choose from but they picked me."

Aubrey caught his breath. He'd been picked too, and, like Moses, he'd been lucky. The day that Molly and Jeremy walked into Sunny Banks Rescue Centre had been the luckiest of his life, and he knew it. Most of the cats he knew had been banged up in a rescue centre at one time or another and for the most part they had nearly all got lucky as well. Apart from Vincent, he thought. There was a sadness in Vincent that Aubrey could never quite fathom. And as close as he and Vincent were, he had never felt that he could really ask him about it.

He listened as Moses continued talking.

"And then one day, David and Stewart said that we were all going to live somewhere else and they showed me some pictures of a house with lots of rooms and they were really happy, so I was happy too. And then there were these men here putting things in big boxes and they were playing music really loudly and I got frightened. They'd left the front door open and I ran out. I thought I'd come back after dark when they were gone and it was safe." His little face wrinkled in distress. "But I couldn't find my way home. I was walking around for days and days."

Aubrey's heart smote him. The mental image of the little cat wandering around, confused and looking for home was hard to bear. But it probably hadn't been for days. Moses's sense of time was about as good as his sense of direction. Although, he corrected himself, he had led them to this house so maybe he had been wandering around for days. He listened as Moses continued.

"And then," said Moses. "One day, I thought that if I climbed up onto a wall, I would be up high. I might be able to see our house again and I'd know where it was."

Aubrey looked at Moses with renewed respect. It was good reasoning by anybody's standards. By Moses standards it was practically genius.

"So what happened?" he asked. "Couldn't you find a high enough wall?"

Moses shook his head.

"No. So I climbed up a tree instead. But before I had a chance to get a good look, some magpies came at me, suddenly, out of nowhere, lots of them, making a horrible noise and flapping their wings at my head. I lost my balance and fell onto some broken glass. It really hurt," he added.

Nasty, thought Aubrey. Broken glass was a real hazard for dogs and cats alike. Their tender paws were easily ripped to ribbons by a carelessly thrown bottle. It wasn't such a problem as it used to be, but it still existed, particularly in those places where people went to drink unobserved. He'd only just managed to avoid a shard of glass himself recently. Glinting in the sunlight, he'd spotted the broken bottle lying by the bin area round the back of the flats just in time. He knew who'd left it there, of course. It was one of the group of men and women who clustered together in the shadows after dark. They slept there as well sometimes, gathering their carrier bags and shopping trolleys around them and moving silently on at daybreak. They were all right for the most part. They didn't bother him and he didn't bother them. But he did wish they'd throw their empties into a bin and not on the ground.

"So what happened next?" asked Vincent.

"I didn't know what to do so I just sat down. And then this boy found me and he looked at my collar and then he took me home."

Aubrey smiled.

"I bet David and Stewart were pleased to see you."

Moses shook his head.

"No. They weren't here. Everything was gone."

"So what happened? How did you end up in that bag?"

"There was a woman here," said Moses. "The boy knocked on the door and she opened it and started shouting. There was a man here, too. And he put me in the bag."

For several minutes all three cats fell silent. Aubrey was well aware of all that nonsense about cats having nine lives. He knew very well that they had just the one, and that one was all too often cut short. Sometimes by accident, like cars hitting them. At other times by negligence and neglect. And sometimes by outright cruelty, which was the worst of all outcomes. At least when a car hit you it was quick.

All that the man had to do, thought Aubrey, was ring a rescue centre. Or contact the previous owners of the flat, presumably he knew where they'd gone. Alternatively, given that Moses wasn't his responsibility, he could have simply refused to take him in. But he hadn't. He had deliberately chosen an act of cruelty. The woman was almost certainly in on it too. She must have known what he was doing. It was no wonder that Moses had such a capacity for happiness. He'd seen the other side, in a way that he, Aubrey, never had. He'd had some hard times, there was no denying that, but he'd never been injured and then thrown away like rubbish.

He looked round, startled at the sound of a cough. The men must be back. That bloke hadn't been kidding when he said that they wouldn't be long. A man strode into the room, his eyes fixed on the phone he was holding and totally failing to notice the three cats in the room.

"Quick, under the covers," he whispered to Vincent and Moses. "Then back to the window."

Silently the three cats dived under the sheets that draped the furniture and then began to edge their way towards the kitchen door.

Outside they gathered round the fish pond again. Out here they were free. They couldn't be trapped, not least because there were two trees, both of which all three of them could scale in seconds. Aubrey stared down at the fish again. There was something very restful about watching them flick in and out of the lily pads. And restful was what he needed after hearing the story that Moses had just told.

He looked down at his little friend now. He appeared his

usual self again, thank goodness. Hopefully he'd already forgotten all about it.

He turned to Vincent.

"Vin, you know that man that just came in."

Vincent nodded.

"Well, he looks sort of familiar. Like I've seen him somewhere before."

"You have," said Vincent. "We all have. He goes to Alfonso's."

CHAPTER THIRTY

C arlos pulled the roasting tin out of the oven and basted the lamb. A lovely aroma of rosemary and garlic drifted around him. It was the first proper Sunday roast that they'd had in months and he was looking forward to it. He glanced at his new phone which lay on the work surface next to him. He hadn't bothered trying to find his old phone. It was quite old and the battery was rubbish, it wouldn't have been too long before he replaced it anyway. And as Jeremy said, it had probably dropped onto the track when he fell, which meant that, by now, a number of trains had probably crushed it out of existence.

Luckily, the insurance that Jeremy had persuaded him to take out had paid up without demur, so he hadn't been too long without a mobile. But at present this new one still felt unfamiliar, like a new pair of trainers before he wore them in. He found it strangely unsettling. But at least he'd still got some of his contacts, including Teddy's, which he'd got from Molly and Jeremy's phones, and his pictures were stored in the cloud so that was all right. The ones that he'd taken in Brighton were really lovely.

He let his mind drift back to that day. It had been perfect in every respect, until he had tumbled onto the train track on the way home. At Jeremy's insistence, he had reported it to the police, but he could tell by the way the kindly officers had looked at him that they didn't believe him, and he wasn't sure that he blamed them. He'd even started to doubt it himself. It had all happened so quickly. He'd probably been mistaken. It had been, surely, just a random nudge, an accidental shove as people jostled for space. The platform had been packed and he'd been standing right on the edge. It must have been, as one of the police officers had said, an accident. They would, he had promised, check the CCTV footage, but it was unlikely that they'd find anything. It was unfortunate, but these things did happen.

He still hadn't told Teddy about it. He had fully intended to but had then changed his mind. While he normally shared everything with her, he didn't want to upset her. And also, as he acknowledged to himself, he didn't want her memory of their Brighton day, as he called it, spoilt. He'd tell her eventually, just not yet.

She was on study leave from university this week, he knew. Perhaps this evening he'd WhatsApp her and catch up on what she'd been doing today. He picked his phone up and rapidly took several snaps of the roasting lamb before he put it back in the oven. Taking photographs of the food he was cooking was something that he'd taken to doing lately, even those dishes that were less successful. Afterwards he transferred them to a digital album with brief notes. He'd read somewhere that many famous chefs kept meticulous notes of recipes that they tried, even the failures. He was doing the twenty-first century equivalent and it was all part of the journey towards his dream restaurant.

He looked up as Jeremy wandered in.

"That smells good. I've just had a call from Teddy's

mother," he said. "She's been trying to ring Teddy but she's having some difficulty or other."

"What did she want?" asked Carlos.

"She wanted to know what time you'd be back."

"Back from where?"

Carlos felt confused. He hadn't gone anywhere so why did they want to know when he'd be back? Anyway, it was Sunday. He nearly always spent Sundays with Molly and Jeremy. It was a lovely comfortable habit that they'd fallen into in recent years. They'd usually go for a short walk, sometimes the cats joined them, then he'd cook lunch and afterwards all of them, including the cats, flopped out in front of the television.

"Apparently Teddy told her yesterday that she was meeting you and then staying overnight somewhere. Only she promised that she'd be back by mid-morning because they've got their monthly family Zoom meeting and some of her cousins that she hasn't seen for ages are joining it. I told her that you were here, at home. That you'd been here all weekend."

"So why did she think that we'd been away?"

Carlos frowned and then felt his stomach suddenly lurch forward. He and Teddy had never stayed away overnight, although they had sometimes talked about it. And if she was just seeing a friend, why would she lie about it and say that she was with him? Teddy never told lies. At least, he didn't think she did. The what-ifs slowly slithered into his thoughts and flicked their forked tongues. What if she was meeting somebody that she didn't want her mum and dad to know about? What if it was somebody they wouldn't approve of? What if it was, like, one of her lecturers or something, and she just said it was him because it was easier? He cast a stricken look at Jeremy.

"You don't think..."

Jeremy pulled back a kitchen chair and sat down.

"No, I don't. Don't panic. Teddy's mum has probably got it

wrong. I expect Teddy went somewhere with a friend and her mum thought that it was you, that's all."

Carlos glanced across at Jeremy. It was late afternoon and a gentle snoring sound permeated the room. Lunch had been particularly good, even if he did say so himself, and the three large glasses of red wine that Jeremy had enjoyed with it had sent him off into a deep slumber. Carlos felt pleased. Jeremy looked so peaceful stretched out in the chair like that. He worked hard at Sir Franks – too hard – and lately he had seemed particularly stressed. That teacher dying hadn't helped. He'd heard him telling Molly that he was having the devil's own job in filling her post.

He watched Jeremy's nose twitch as he made himself more comfortable. It was good to see him so relaxed. If only he could feel that way himself. Today had started so well. He'd woken in a good mood and sprung out of bed, already planning the timings for the lunch he was going to cook. Since he'd been working full time he understood the value of weekends in a way that he hadn't before and he'd been looking forward to the day ahead. And now a dark cloud loomed over him and he felt a sense of dread that he just couldn't shift. Even with the comforting weight of Aubrey on his lap he could feel the filaments of anxiety threading through him.

He had tried to reassure himself while they ate lunch. Jeremy was probably right. Teddy's mum had got confused. She'd probably mixed up their day trip to Brighton with some other thing that Teddy had told her. Because Teddy wouldn't cheat on him, she wouldn't just go off with someone else. She wouldn't do that to him, no matter how many posh university boys she met. She just wouldn't. Would she?

But that was what Rubble had thought about his girlfriend, Kylie. He'd thought that they would stay together forever. He'd confided in Carlos that he intended to marry her as soon as he finished college and had even gone so far as to start saving for an engagement ring. That day in the student common room when Kylie had told him that she was now going out with someone else, he had stood up and walked out with leaden feet, pale-faced and unable to speak. In the end he had just gone home and nobody had seen him for the next three days. That was the first and only time that Carlos had ever known Rubble to be less than cheerful, although in true Rubble fashion it hadn't taken him too long to bounce back. But he wasn't like Rubble. He would never bounce back from losing Teddy. If he didn't have Teddy, almost everything else became meaningless. Who cared about dream restaurants if there was no Teddy to share it with?

He felt in his pocket for his phone and stared down at the screen. He had decided that after lunch he would ring her. He would wait that long because, surely, she would be home by then. But now he had his doubts. They didn't often talk on the phone, preferring text and WhatsApp, and ringing her now didn't seem like such a good idea anymore. It would feel like he was checking up on her, which he was, and his instinct told him that would be a bad move. But what would be a good move? He had absolutely no idea. He and Teddy had always trusted each other and to introduce any element of doubt would cast a long shadow. But he couldn't just do nothing.

Perhaps he could send her a short text, just sort of saying hello or something, but Teddy was nothing if not intuitive. She would know that he wasn't just saying hello. She would know that the subtext was him asking where she was and who she was with, and he knew that she wouldn't like it. The best thing to do would be to ask Molly, she always knew about this sort of thing. He stood up and then stopped as she walked into the room. He felt his heart start to pound. Something had happened. He could tell by the look on her face.

"Carlos, don't panic."

He started towards her and she held up her hand.

"No, sit down." She waited until he sat down again and then sat next to him. "I've just had a call from Teddy's mother."

Carlos felt his throat go dry and he swallowed hard. He tried to speak but his mouth felt numb. From across the room Jeremy stirred. Rubbing his eyes, he sat up and looked at them.

"What's up with you two?" he said. "Looks like you've lost a pound and found a penny, as my granny used to say."

He sat up straighter and looked at them more closely.

"What is it? What's happened?"

"It's Teddy," said Molly.

"What about her?"

Jeremy was wide awake now, his earlier sleepiness completely evaporated.

Molly hesitated for a second and ran her tongue over her bottom lip before speaking.

"She seems to be missing."

Carlos swallowed and tried to force some words out but none came.

"How do you know?" asked Jeremy.

"Her mother has just been on the phone. When she couldn't contact her she tried some of her university friends, but none of them have heard from her. According to Teddy's mother, she went out yesterday afternoon and nobody has seen her since."

Carlos sat hunched on the little armchair that he had brought with him from the flat that he had lived in with his mother and which now stood in his bedroom. Along his shoulders Aubrey lay draped, his tail looped loosely around his neck. Any compunction Carlos had felt earlier about ringing Teddy had completely evaporated. For the hundredth time he pressed her number. For the hundredth time there was nothing. Something dreadful had happened, he was sure of it. Teddy was close to her parents. She would never just disappear without telling them, especially as she'd promised to be at home for the family Zoom meeting. He closed his eyes briefly but the unwelcome images crowded in on him and he opened them again.

There were reports every day in the press and on television about girls being harmed, and university students seemed to be particularly vulnerable. Free of parental constraints and living more or less independently for the first time, they often seemed to take foolish risks. But not Teddy. She was free-spirited and carefree and he loved her for it, but she wasn't a fool. She was the very last person to get in a car with a stranger, or take a shortcut through a park at night. No, if Teddy was missing it was because she'd had an accident. Or something worse. He didn't care now who she was with or what she'd been doing. He cared only that she was safe and well and that no harm had come to her.

He dipped his head as he felt his throat tighten. It was all very well Molly and Jeremy telling him that there was almost certainly nothing to worry about, that Teddy would turn up as right as rain, whatever that meant. Their words were kindly meant and intended to comfort him, he knew that, but unlike most boys of his age he also knew that disasters weren't confined to the movies. Bad things happened, and they happened for real. He had experienced tragedy up close and personal.

CHAPTER THIRTY-ONE

Teddy pushed her back more tightly against the wall and pulled her legs up, her mind fogged with fear and uncertainty. Up until now she had thought that she was a girl who could cope with anything, that she and her friends would always have a plan no matter what. Seven of them in total, they had met at primary school and pretty much stuck together ever since. Not a week went by when one or other of them didn't message their WhatsApp group. She wondered what they were doing now. Drinking coffee? Getting ready to go out? Whatever it was, it was fairly certain that they weren't sitting alone and afraid in a place that they didn't recognise.

They had been Brownies and then Guides together and away on camp they had sat outside their tents at night toasting marshmallows and inventing more and more improbable adventures in which they each took heroic parts. They'd even made a medal from an old brooch, which one of them had pinched from her mother, and awarded it to the best storyteller. On her last camp she had won it and she still had it now, resting at the bottom of her treasure box. Her story, if she recalled correctly, involved being taken hostage during a bank raid and held while the robber tried to negotiate with the police who were massed outside.

She felt a sudden pang. How naïve they all were. So sure that in whatever situation they found themselves, each and every one of them would have the resources to find their way out. After all, they had been Girl Guides and they had the badges to prove it. Now, faced with reality, she had no answers. Only questions.

It felt chilly in here now, and she clasped her hands around her knees and dropped her head. She had no idea what the time was, there was no signal on her phone, but she had definitely slept at one point so perhaps she had been here all night. She raised her head again and reached into the small backpack lying next to her. The water bottle that her mother insisted that she and Casper always carry when they were out and about felt comforting in her hand. They had often groaned about it, but she was glad of it now. She took a long cool draught and wiped her hand across her mouth.

She had been surprised to get the message. Not surprised that Carlos had messaged her, but surprised that it had come from his old phone. He'd told her that he had lost it but presumably it had turned up somewhere and he was using up any remaining credit. It's what she would have done. But had she got the place wrong? She couldn't check on her phone but surely she hadn't? She had followed his instructions to the letter, thrilled that he'd laid a kind of treasure trail of clues to take her to a place where a surprise awaited her. After that, he was going to take her to a small hotel that he'd found and which he knew she would love. The latter suggestion had surprised her. Although they had sometimes talked about spending time away together, talking was about as far as they'd got. He must have found somewhere really special to suggest it now.

She took another draught of water and looked around her.

What this place was, she didn't have a clue. It was like a huge room, but not like any room that she had ever been in before. It didn't have any windows, for a start. Big boxes and crates were stacked along two of the walls and she had been tempted to peer inside them. In the end she had resisted. She might find something that she didn't want to see. It was bad enough that she was locked in here, she didn't need her imagination racking up overtime. The rest of the space was just cavernous and empty, apart from a shabby little sofa with a pine dining table next to it, the ring marks from hot mugs still evident on its surface. Luckily she had spotted a light switch hanging from a thin cord. The single dim bulb meant that at least she wasn't sitting in total darkness.

She got up and stretched. Her legs felt awkward and, conscious of the stiffness in her muscles and joints, she moved slowly towards the door. Reaching out she hammered against it again, her small fists pounding the unyielding surface. It was no good. It was as firmly shut as it had been the last time. She ran her fingers over the lock. When Casper was younger he had been given a little wooden money box, complete with money, with a lock which he had managed to open using their mother's tweezers. But she didn't have any tweezers and, anyway, this lock looked rather more robust than the one on Casper's money box. She had heard the firm click as whoever was on the other side had turned the key. How long would it take, she wondered, to use up all the oxygen in a space like this? Hours? Days? Weeks? She had no idea. Leaning forward she rested her forehead against the cold metal, struggling against the tears that threatened to fall.

She hadn't got it wrong, she was sure that she hadn't. The instructions that Carlos had given had simply said to get off the train at the usual station and then instead of heading for his house, turn right away from the town and then walk along a rough track towards what looked like a deserted yard. She would know that she was in the right place because about halfway along there would be a blue ribbon tied to the branch of one of the young saplings that had planted itself there.

She had walked slowly, watching for the blue ribbon and savouring the peace and the stillness. It felt like a million miles away from the hustle and bustle of the town. To one side lay a disused railway track and she had marvelled at the resilience of the wildflowers and plants that grew there, rampant and strong among the rusting abandoned trucks still parked on the rails.

On the other side of the tracks was an old biscuit factory, long since closed, its faded lettering still visible on the red Victorian brick. It had been many years now since it had made biscuits for anybody and she could see the big hoarding next to it proclaiming the exciting new development for luxury apartments that was scheduled for the new year. She had paused and stared at it for a moment, imagining all the workers bustling in and out of the factory gates and the aroma of fresh baking filtering out across the railway line. It was sad that it was no longer in operation, but better that it should be preserved and made into new homes, better than it being demolished altogether. Her father had told her that often happened to the old Victorian factories and warehouses in the nineteen sixties and it had made her feel sad. It was as though all the lives and hopes and dreams of those that had worked in them had never been.

She had looked again at the rusting rail trucks and smiled to herself. Casper had told her only recently of an abandoned railway line somewhere in the west country where a number of people had seen a ghost locomotive chugging along, a report of which had prompted him to expand the Beaumont International Detective Agency to include supernatural investigations. It was, he had assured her, where the real money was. She had resisted the temptation to point out that as he hadn't made any money at all from the detective agency, real or otherwise, it was all rather immaterial. Casper was a total arse on occasion, but he was her little brother, and she loved him dearly. And at least playing at detectives kept him out of trouble. More or less. She had pulled her phone out and taken a photograph of the track and sent it to him. He'd like that.

On reaching the yard and holding the blue ribbon that she had plucked from the sapling, she had opened the small wooden gate and looked for the spray of roses which Carlos had said would indicate where she was to go. And there it had been. A small bouquet of pink roses was laid before the door of what looked like a huge metal box, one of a number lined up against the far side of the yard. She had run towards it, eager to find out what Carlos had planned. She guessed that it would be something to do with food. Perhaps he had made a special meal or picnic and had laid the table inside for just the two of them, probably with a table cloth and candles. Knowing Carlos, he would have printed a menu too. She hoped so. She could save it, along with all her other mementos. She had picked up the roses and pushed open the door, blinking rapidly as her eyes adjusted from the autumn sunshine outside to the gloom of the interior. And then she had heard it. The clanging shut of the door followed by a small quiet cough. She had spun round, expecting to see Carlos standing smiling before her. She had been quite alone.

She walked back across the floor and slid down into her previous position. The phrase 'back to the wall', she suddenly realised, had a real meaning. If you had your back to the wall you could see all around you. Nobody could come at you by surprise. But why would anybody want to? Anyway, Carlos was the only person who knew that she was here. She hadn't told anybody where she was going because she hadn't known herself until she had got here. A horrible thought struck her. What if it hadn't been Carlos who had sent the message? What if somebody had found his phone and tricked her into coming here? But why would they? The inside of her mouth felt suddenly dry. Maybe somebody was coming to get her. Maybe it was like one of those horror films that she sometimes watched with Casper, where the victim was lured away to meet a terrible fate. A bolt of terror shot through her and she found herself struggling to breathe. In a space like this there was nowhere to run. Nowhere to hide. She could scream all she liked. Nobody would hear her. She pressed her hand against her chest and briefly closed her eyes, forcing herself to take slow deep breaths.

She was being silly, she knew she was. The message must have come from Carlos. Some random stranger who'd picked up his phone wouldn't know where he lived, which station he used, where his house was. But Carlos wouldn't try to frighten her, surely, even as a joke. He wasn't like that. Although some boys could be very cruel, Carlos wasn't one of them. He wasn't like some of those boys that her friends had told her about, boys who arranged dates with them and then didn't show up. Or, even worse, did show up but brought their mates with them and laughed. Those were the same sort of boys who wrote rude and disparaging comments about girls appearance on their social media posts, calling them fat and ugly and often much worse. But not Carlos. Even if Carlos was upset or angry he wouldn't do anything like this. Not to her, not to anybody And anyway, why would he be upset or angry with her? The last time they had met had been in Brighton and they'd had a lovely time. They'd both agreed that it was about their best day, ever. Anyway, they'd WhatsApp'd since then and there had been no hint of anything untoward. If Carlos was upset or hurt about anything, he would tell her. She was sure of it.

But his hadn't been an easy path in life, she was aware of

that, and these things take their toll. She had asked him once about his childhood, curious to know more about where he had come from. His response had been the plain unembellished truth and it had shocked her. Brazil is, he had told her, a beautiful country, truly beautiful, but it had its dark side just like every other country.

Born into poverty, he had lived in a cramped apartment in a district riddled with gangs and crime. With him had lived his mother, his fading and confused grandfather, and his unpredictable and volatile alcoholic father. His mother had been the one to provide for them all. She had worked all hours at any job she could get, determined to lift them out of poverty and get him away to England. As a result he had arrived in the United Kingdom as an illegal immigrant. Living as unobtrusively as they could in the sub-let council flat that he and his mother had unlawfully occupied, they had waited in dread for the knock on the door which surely must come. The dream of the better life in England that his mother had hoped and prayed for had in reality been a struggle for an existence that was barely better than the one they had in Brazil. In some respects it had been even worse. At least in Brazil they were entitled to be there. And then, just when he'd been settled in school and things were beginning to look as though they might improve, his mother had been brutally murdered. Not only that, Carlos had been the one to find her.

For the first time she found herself wondering what might have happened if the Goodmans hadn't taken Carlos in when they had. It was something that she had never really thought about before, so accustomed was she to Carlos being part of the Goodman family. She didn't know, but she suspected that young teenagers left on their own were not usually given much choice. The authorities would have stepped in, the cogs of the system would have started whirring, and that would have been that. Carlos would have simply been an inconvenient statistic and would no doubt have ended up in some care home. As soon as he was deemed old enough he would have been chucked out onto the street to fend for himself the best way he could. She knew about teenagers like that.

Her father was a magistrate who also sat in the youth court. In theory they had support. In fact they often fell through the cracks, the unseen victims of an overburdened state. Her father had told her about the depressing ease with which these boys and girls slipped under the radar and then fell into a life of crime. Having no family and lacking any status elsewhere, they turned to older criminals and gang members for some kind of validity. In the worst cases they were the kind of youths who ended up dying alone on the street, their early demise the result of knife or gun. She shuddered slightly. She was well aware that by comparison her own life had been positively gilded. Neither she nor Casper had ever wanted for anything. They had known nothing but warmth, comfort and security all their lives.

Vivid as her imagination undoubtedly was, she struggled to think what life must have been really like for Carlos before the Goodmans. Truth to tell, she often forgot that he wasn't their natural son. He always seemed so – what her mother would have called – well-adjusted. It was hard to imagine him in any other environment than the one he now occupied. But perhaps all the trauma that he had experienced had been festering under the surface all along. Perhaps at last it had erupted and thrown his mind into chaos. It would hardly be surprising, given everything that he had endured. She thought about his open, honest face with its beautiful dark eyes and soft expressive mouth, and felt her eyes fill again. Carlos would never do anything to hurt her. He just wouldn't. He wasn't like those other boys.

She raised her head suddenly as a thought struck her.

Perhaps Carlos had been held up in some way. Perhaps some last minute emergency or something had delayed him. He wouldn't know that she couldn't get a signal on her phone. He'd probably been trying to ring her. Her heart lifted and then sank again. The door of the room had been shut and locked firmly behind her. She had heard the reverberating clank as it closed and the harsh click of the key in the lock. It had been no invisible hand that had done that. She felt her throat constrict again as the tears started to fall.

CHAPTER THIRTY-TWO

He pulled up outside the apartment and sat for a moment, thinking. Things were very close to the end now, but with it that brought a strange feeling of regret. He had thought he would feel differently, a sense of relief, a euphoric freedom that he'd won, but he didn't. What he really felt was a longing to do it all again. It was something that he hadn't expected, He knew what had done it, of course. It was that moment he had shoved Carlos in the back. The rush of excitement, the thrill of the power of life and death quite literally in his hands was addictive. He had to let it go, he knew. He couldn't risk everything that he'd achieved, not now. But still those scorpions scuttled in, scurrying around and disturbing his peace of mind. He shook the thoughts away. He'd think about it later. In the meantime there was still Teddy to deal with.

He had originally planned to text her, a really unpleasant one, but somehow that didn't quite do it. It wasn't enough, he had wanted something that would not only shock but really upset her. Something that would jolt her out of her cosy little life. The problem was that he couldn't quite work out what that might be. He could always send some images he supposed, but no sooner had he thought of the idea than he dismissed it. Apart from the fact that he would have to search for them, thereby risking himself to exposure, there was something... he searched for the right word. Inartistic. That was it. Images were inartistic. There was no creativity involved. Although the impact was instant, they were one dimensional. Once seen they were more easily dismissed. Words were different. He could control words. He could use them any way he wanted. Words were, by their nature, open to interpretation. Choose the right ones and they were capable of leaving a lingering poison long after they had been read.

But as satisfying as composing such a message might be, he really wanted something that would result in more of an ordeal. He liked the word ordeal. So much so that he'd looked it up. It meant to go through something difficult and painful. That's what he'd wanted for her. Something difficult and painful. He'd been stuck, until he thought of the container. If he said so himself, and he did, the container idea was a stroke of genius. The more he thought about it, the more he liked it. Lockable, secure, and with no phone signal the container was the ideal place. Thank goodness he still had it. He had kept meaning to let it go, it had been at the back of his mind for some time, along with the other things that he needed to get rid of, but he was glad now that he hadn't.

He had originally rented the container to store the things that he had taken away from his parents' house after his mother died. The kitchen equipment, the crockery, the cutlery, the framed but unglazed prints that had hung on the walls, he had donated all of those to local charities. But the cheap furniture the local charities hadn't wanted. He wasn't surprised. It was mostly stuff that his parents had bought when they were first married and they had more than had their money's worth out of it. In the end he'd hired a van and taken most of it to the tip.

There had still been a surprising amount left though and, even more surprisingly, he had been reluctant to dispose of certain items. He had thought that he wouldn't be able to wait to see the back of it all, but he had been wrong.

When it had come to it, he had been loath to get rid of the cheap pine dining table that his father had sat at while he tried to balance the unbalanceable books. He had felt the same about the battered little sofa that had stood under the window in the front room and on which he had jumped up and down when he was a small boy. And then there were the books. Hundreds and hundreds of them, barely opened and, if read, certainly not by anyone in his family. But they were testament to the fact, in the unlikely event that anybody should ever be interested, that as a family they were worth something. They had books. His father had collected them over the years from second-hand bookshops and library sales, with the hardbacks always being more prized than the paperbacks, no matter the subject matter. It was funny, he thought. He had despised those books when he was growing up, he had found their existence somehow embarrassing, but when it came to it, he had been strangely reluctant to get rid of them. So now they sat in their crates, all those biographies of long-forgotten politicians and lawyers crammed in with cheap romantic fiction and histories of the British navy.

In the years since his parents had died, having a container had been a strange comfort to him. It had been a kind of buffer against the outside world. It was his own kingdom and it was the place where he kept his notes. Small paper exercise books that he had stolen from the stationery cupboard at primary school, they were the testament to his dreams. Since the age of nine he had used them to meticulously plan and chart his way through life and they were precious. They were the validation of his very existence. Every scheme, even those he hadn't managed to accomplish successfully, had been mapped out in those books.

Dated and updated, they had accompanied him over the years and it was his secret pleasure to fish them out from where they were hidden, tucked well into the centre of one of the crates of books between *The Life of Mr Justice Swift* and *A Popular History of the Great War*. Poring over them brought him a kind of inner peace that nothing else, not even a bottle of single malt, could match.

When he had moved to this town he had simply let the first container go and rented another one. He had completed all transactions under an assumed name. He wasn't entirely sure why, other than that he had wanted it to be private, something that was just for him. The container was something that nobody could interfere with and something that nobody else could access other than the owner. Approached by foot from a rough track which ran along the side of the disused railway and by car from a small side road which ran along the other side of the railway, it sat with the other containers. A solid steel space with no windows and a good old-fashioned sturdy lock, with a big padlock for good measure, both of which looked more than sufficient to deter any opportunistic thief.

He had paid for his containers annually, using money orders which he had obtained using cash. There were no ID checks, no requirement for proof of address or anything like that. There hadn't even been a written agreement. The only time that he had visited the owner's office had been to pick up the keys and he had been handed them by a bored looking boy who had barely glanced at him, being more interested in flicking through his phone. The chances of the boy remembering him were remote to say the least.

There was, he knew, something about the idea of secure storage that appealed to him. Ever since he was a boy he had kept secrets. Some were big secrets, such as the time he had seen a neighbour with her mouth locked against that of a man who most definitely was not her husband. Other secrets were not so big, such as witnessing his father hiding in the back room and eating chocolate bars from the shop. He had watched from the shadows with a mixture of pity and contempt. Apart from the fact that his father was pilfering his own stock, which was not a great idea considering the profit margin was already practically non-existent, he was a diabetic. He'd said nothing, either to the neighbour or his father, but he had felt bolstered by his knowledge. Secrets were his small pleasure and he held them close. They made him feel not only important but safe. They were a kind of insurance. An insurance against what he didn't know, but he felt it instinctively.

The container, as well as being his secret, was a safe space for him to inhabit. It was lockable and secure, something which nobody else would ever know about, and this one, his second, was even better than the first. It was bigger and more remote and he visited it regularly. The point was that nobody who was looking for him would ever find him there. Even his phone lost its signal as soon as he shut the door. Sometimes he slipped a half bottle of whisky into his pocket and just sat on his parents' cheap sofa, thinking and drinking. Occasionally he opened a box or crate and peered inside.

The very smell of the contents always carried him back, evoking memories of small town life and small-minded people. He didn't feel any nostalgia or misplaced sentiment, just relief that he was no longer there. He wasn't sorry that his parents were no longer alive. They'd had nothing to look forward to but an uncomfortable old age in which they would be permanently fretting about the heating bills. And all the time the weight of the unspoken expectation of his offer of help would be hanging over him. After all, he was their only child and he owed them something. It was his duty. They would never have actually said it but it would have been there, simmering away, occasionally surfacing with a throwaway remark on how glad they were that they knew they could always rely on him, followed by a sharp glance and an uncomfortable silence.

Would he have made such an offer? Would he, for instance, have had them to live with him? He knew that he wouldn't. While he was well aware that many elderly people lived long and healthy lives, many others didn't and were forced to rely on carers of one sort or another to help them cope with the most basic of everyday tasks. As his parents had moved slowly forward from their middle years towards old age it had seemed to him that they had started to diminish. They had already started the long goodbye.

Even before he had collapsed with the heart attack that had killed him, his father had become a little vague, a little less certain, while the spectacle of his mother disintegrating before his eyes over such a short space of time had frankly terrified him. Had she not died when she did, it wouldn't have been too long before she was unable to even wash and dress herself and the role of carer was not one that he had been prepared to assume.

He didn't think less well of himself because of that. In his opinion, people of his parents' generation simply didn't know what they were asking when they blithely assumed that they would live with their children if the need arose. The truth was that they had escaped the worst of it. Previous generations had been less long-lived and many people had died well before any senility or real frailness set in. In the case of his own grandparents, both sets had died when they were still in their sixties and early seventies, which he now realised was fairly young, although they had seemed old to him at the time. But the point was that his mother and father hadn't been forced to witness the slow unravelling of them, or had the anxiety of dealing with the chaos that dragged in its wake. Having aged and infirm parents to live with would, he thought, be like having small children in the house. But they were small children that would never grow up. He wouldn't ever have agreed to it, he knew that he wouldn't, no matter how much pressure he had been put under, and even if his mother hadn't suffered from Alzheimer's. He'd known it then and he knew it now. He might have sent them some money from time to time but that would have been about the extent of it. Anyway, all that was over now. He didn't need to think about it ever again. They were gone and that was that.

CHAPTER THIRTY-THREE

H e leaned forward slightly as he pulled the cork on the bottle of wine, and then glanced at his watch. Jeannie would be here soon. Neil was travelling up north on some business trip and had decided to drive there today to avoid the Monday rush, so she would come over as soon as he had left. It would be three weeks before the new tenants moved in so they still had the apartment to themselves for the time being, which was great. He let out a long sigh of satisfaction. In all, this had turned out to be a very good weekend with everything going according to plan.

He had laid the whole operation carefully, chosen his words, set the bait, but he was well aware that it was hit-and-miss. He knew from the texts that Teddy and Carlos had exchanged that Teddy was studying at university, so she was no fool. She might easily have seen through the whole thing straight away. But he needn't have worried. In the end, getting her there had been laughably easy. She had fallen for it hook, line and proverbial sinker. He smiled to himself. These teenagers, so wise, so world weary. So pathetic. They thought they knew everything and they knew nothing. Particularly girls, with their heads full of notions about love and romance. You'd think that they would know better these days, but no. They were just as silly as they'd always been. Even the clever ones. Trail a few ribbons and roses and they would blindly follow wherever they were led, as he had just proved.

He pulled the phone out of his inside pocket and looked at it with narrowed eyes. It would be foolish to switch it on, even though he thought it was extremely unlikely that anybody was still looking for it, but it was no good, he couldn't resist. He comforted himself with the thought that even if it was tracked here to Jeannie's apartment, this place had nothing to do with him. Nobody could link him with it. He been careful throughout, reading all of Carlos's texts and messages during a train trip he'd taken for that specific purpose. He'd been rather pleased with himself about that. He wasn't sure exactly how it worked, but his guess was that the signal must have been pinging off masts in about three different counties. Good luck to whoever tried to trace that. Again, that was supposing that anybody was actually looking, which he doubted. The message that he had sent to Teddy had been written while he was sitting in a crowded pizza place on the other side of town where every other person in there had their phone out. But this would be the last time he turned it on. Positively the last time. After today he would take a hammer to it.

He ran his thumb over the screen and read the messages again. This girl Teddy and Carlos were obviously in love, judging by their stupid messages. He sneered slightly. He hadn't ever been in love himself, not in the whole of his life. As far as he was concerned being in love was some construct, some notion dreamed up by the advertisers and PR people who flogged it to the plebs so they would buy their stupid products. It was true that he'd been quite fond of various girls and women over the years, he was fond of Jeannie in his own way, they suited each other, but he had never felt that all-consuming emotion that the films and novels portrayed. He didn't care. He didn't think that he'd missed anything. He only had to look back on some of his old school friends, the ones that had married when they were barely out of their teens, to see where romance got you.

He'd decided early on that wasn't to be the life for him but he'd been astute enough to pretend that he had felt love when it had suited him, and he thought that generally he had played the part well. Just as he always played any part well. But it had always been for his own gain. There had always been something in it for him. Like his very first girlfriend, Ivy.

He thought of her now. A tall, quite pretty girl in an outdoorsy way, with long, straight, fair hair whose old-fashioned name had suited her. She had certainly clung to him, that was for sure. She wasn't particularly clever, it hadn't taken him long to work that out, but she did have a certain something. Most importantly, she was popular and in with all the right kids. Before long he was popular and in with all the right kids, too. It was an early lesson and he'd learned it well. Surround yourself with the right props, be that people or things, and anything was achievable. But the relationship with Ivy hadn't lasted. Her mother and father hadn't liked him and eventually she had entwined herself around someone else. Her parents dislike of him was pure prejudice on their part, he had known it, but it hadn't bothered him. He'd got what he wanted. Love was for fools. Where did it get you? Nowhere that he wanted to go, he was certain of that.

He changed screen and stared again at the pictures of the laughing girl and felt his mouth harden. Something about her just incited his inner rage. He could tell that she was posh just by looking at her. She had one of those round faces with bright sparkling eyes and pretty white teeth, with that annoying air of confident self-assurance which told her that she would be welcome anywhere that she went. In thirty years' time, she would be cutting the ribbon at the local fete. The ice chips in his heart hardened. It was all luck of the draw. Born wealthy. Born poor. The die was cast from the moment you opened your eyes.

He looked at the most recent picture of her. She had been standing on a railway platform just about to board a train and had turned and waved, presumably at Carlos as it was his phone that had been used to take the picture. Young and free, with not a care in the world, a broad smile had been lighting up her lovely face. She had the kind of skin that was the product of being fed home-made meals packed with fresh fruit and vegetables, not the unhealthy pallor with accompanying eczema that had been his teenaged complexion and which had been the result of being given out of date ready meals from the shop freezer as his main source of sustenance. Until he was grown up, he hadn't even known that spaghetti didn't have to come in tins. He peered more closely at the date-stamp. It was the day that he had pushed Carlos onto the track. He laughed. If Carlos had been hit by a train that would have wiped the smile off her face.

He flicked back through the other photographs. Lots of them were of plates of food. Weird. Who took pictures of plates of food? Well, obviously Carlos did, but why? You'd think he would have had enough, working all day with it. He pushed the thought away. What did it matter to him? Carlos could take photographs of the soles of his shoes for all he cared. He felt a sudden impulse to write one more letter to Carlos, a really nasty one that would go further than anything he'd written before. He let his thoughts run into free-range mode, savouring the unsavoury possibilities.

He started to compose it in his mind, carefully selecting the right phrases, and then reluctantly deleted it. He'd promised himself that he wouldn't write any more. He'd got away with it so far. It would be reckless to push it any further, but it was a pity. He'd enjoyed writing those letters. What had started as a necessity had become an enjoyable pastime but he needed to delete the file on his computer, just in case. He could save it on a memory stick though. He smiled to himself. It would be something nice to look back on in his old age. And who knew? He might even pick it all up again. When everything had settled down.

He walked over to the window and wondered how Teddy was getting on. She must be thoroughly scared by now, as well as cold and hungry. Well, when he and Jeannie had finished here he might go over and quietly unlock the container. He could bang on the door and then slip round the corner and be out of sight before she'd had time to realise that she was free. Alternatively, he might just leave her there. It would serve her right. What for, he didn't know.

CHAPTER THIRTY-FOUR

Aubrey looked across at Moses and nudged Vincent.

"I see Moses is engaged in his usual study of the natural world."

Vincent glanced over to where Moses was staring intently at a blade of grass.

"Well, it keeps him happy." He studied Moses more closely. "Do you ever wonder what he's thinking about?"

Aubrey laughed.

"No, not really. Come on, let's take him for a walk."

Moses looked up as they approached.

"Why is there so much of it?" he asked.

"So much of what, Moses?" said Aubrey.

"All this," said Moses, and looked vaguely around him at the lawn and flower beds surrounding them.

And that, thought Aubrey, was a rather profound question. Why indeed was there so much of it? It occurred to him that there might actually be more to Moses than they ever gave him credit for. Although, to be fair, it would be hard for there to be less. He looked at Vincent.

"Because," said Vincent gravely. "That's how it's meant to be."

Moses nodded, apparently satisfied with Vincent's explanation.

"Are they all still upset?" he asked.

Aubrey knew what he was talking about. The shadows that had fallen over the Goodman household wrapped around him again. When he had left the house, Teddy still hadn't turned up. He had heard Molly and Jeremy talking in serious tones, deliberately keeping their voices low, and he knew that they were worried. When he had nudged the door open and walked into the room they had stopped talking, until Jeremy had spotted that it was him.

"It's all right, Moll. It's only Aubrey. He won't say anything."

And Molly had nodded and carried on talking.

Trailing upstairs with Vincent, they had found Carlos in his room, motionless in his little armchair, white-faced and silent. He and Vincent had sat with him, both managing to crush onto his lap, but he hadn't appeared to notice their presence, not even reaching down to stroke them. Aubrey had felt a strangeness in the atmosphere until he had realised what that strangeness was. It was the absence of music. In common with many teenagers, Carlos played out his life against a backdrop of music. Even when he was getting ready for bed his phone played music, the constant hum and thrum often sending him off to sleep. This afternoon there had been nothing. The only sound had been that of their collective breathing. Eventually they had slipped back downstairs and out of the cat flap to talk to Moses who was sitting on the lawn.

Moses looked up at his two friends, apparently thinking, although with Moses you could never tell.

"I heard someone crying," he said eventually.

"Did you, Moses?" asked Aubrey. "When was that?"

"Earlier today," said Moses. He dropped his gaze and looked away to his right, his voice lowered. "By the railway."

Aubrey frowned and moved closer.

"Where?"

Moses looked back again and flicked his little paw across his ear before speaking.

"By the railway," he said, his voice clearer this time.

Aubrey sighed. How many times did they have to tell Moses not to go near the railway, unless they were with him? The railway station was fascinating and offered all sorts of opportunity for adventure but it was a dangerous place. Not only was it full of strangers coming and going, but it would be all too easy for a little cat to slip onto the track. And nobody going to risk their life to haul him out, that was for sure. That was if they even noticed that he'd fallen.

"Moses," he started. "How many times do we..."

"Not the big railway," said Moses, interrupting. "The other one."

Aubrey looked at Vincent, puzzled. What other one? There was only one railway station in the town, unless you included the miniature railway in the park, but that only ran in the summer months.

"The one with the quiet trains."

Vincent smiled and turned to Aubrey.

"He means the abandoned tracks."

"Right," said Aubrey. "Well, Moses, I suppose it's all right if you go over there, but you really ought to wait for us. We can take you, you only have to ask."

"You lot were all busy," said Moses simply. "I came in the cat flap and waited around for a while, and then I went away again."

It was true, thought Aubrey. They had all been preoccupied with Teddy's disappearance. He hadn't even heard the cat flap, and neither had Vincent. Normally they could hear the click-clack of it opening and closing at a thousand paces. Had they heard it today they would have been down there in a split second, ready to see off any marauding cat who had the temerity to stray onto their territory, but they had heard nothing.

"This crying," he said, turning to Moses. "Did you see who it was?"

Moses shook his head.

"No, it was coming from one of those big box things."

Aubrey thought for a moment. What big box thing? He gave an inward sigh. The expression 'willing but not very able' could have been invented for Moses.

"What big box thing was that then, Moses?" he asked.

"You know," said Moses. "The big box things."

"He means those container things that people put stuff in. The ones in the yard," said Vincent. He looked more closely at Moses. "Are you sure that was what you heard? Those boxes are meant to store objects in, they're not meant for people."

Moses nodded, his eyes bright.

"Somebody was crying," he repeated. "I heard it."

"Well," said Vincent slowly. "If someone's got shut in one by mistake, there's really not much that we can do about it."

Aubrey thought about it for a moment. Vin was right of course. They'd been in the yard occasionally, it was a great place for ratting, but those big box things were just that. Big boxes. They didn't have any windows or anything. He'd seen inside one once when a woman came to open it. He'd watched as she put her key in the lock and then he'd crept closer as she pulled the door open. He hadn't followed her in though, curious as he had been. His instinct had told him that once inside, if the door closed there would be no way out. If he got trapped in one, then he would stay trapped until somebody opened the door again, and that could be days, months even. By which time he would have starved to death. He felt slightly sick at the thought. Being hungry with no access to food was his worst nightmare. Even if he got hit by a car it would be quick. But left without food... it really didn't bear thinking about.

He looked down at the hopeful little face staring up at him. Moses always assumed that they could solve any problem that he presented them with. And in truth, they usually could. But not this one. This one was beyond them. Those doors needed keys to open them and even if they had a key, they wouldn't be able to use it. Paws were made for lots of things but handling keys wasn't one of them. But there was no harm in them strolling over there. It wasn't like they were doing anything else.

"I suppose we could always go and take a look," he said eventually.

Without waiting for an answer, he turned and slipped quickly under the garden gate, followed by Vincent and Moses. Aubrey watched as Moses scampered happily ahead.

"Do you think he really heard somebody crying?" he asked Vincent.

"I doubt it. It was probably a bird or something. We'll take him over there but we shouldn't hang about for too long. It'll be getting dark soon."

***

The three cats reached the disused railway track and sauntered towards the yard, savouring the stillness of the crisp autumn air and the prospect of hunting in the undergrowth. They should come here more often, Aubrey thought. It was a great place to explore. He turned to Vincent, about to speak, and then stopped. Something was going on. He reached a paw towards Moses to stop him going any further.

Although there was no noise, every instinct told him that they were not alone. Without a word Aubrey and Vincent moved forward, keeping Moses between them. Scrambling up the yard gate they dropped down the other side and stationed themselves among the shrubs and weeds on the far side. In front of one of the boxes a police car was parked, and next to that a small white van. Two police officers stood and watched, their expressions tense as a third man leaned over the door, his back to them. On the ground beside him lay an open case of instruments.

Aubrey turned to Vincent, about to speak, and then swung round as a third vehicle raced into the yard. Aubrey stared. He recognised that car. It belonged to Teddy's father, Jonathon Beaumont. He and Vincent had been in it once when Jeremy's car had broken down and Teddy's father had picked them all up. Jonathon and Casper climbed out of the car.

He turned to Vincent.

"It's Teddy's father and brother. What are they doing here?"

Vincent looked at him, his expression grim.

"I think we can take a guess."

They watched as the man with his back to them continued with his work, pausing occasionally to select another instrument from the case at his feet. They held their breath as he straightened up and faced the police officers.

"Okay, that's it."

The three cats jumped at the roar of yet another car engine. Into the yard burst Carlos, his face covered in sweat and his hair plastered to his forehead.

CHAPTER THIRTY-FIVE

Jonathon Beaumont smiled as Molly passed him a mug of coffee.

"Thanks, Molly. We'll be out of your hair soon. Only, once the police were finished, Teddy was insistent that she wanted to spend some time with Carlos before I took her home."

"It's fine," said Jeremy. "Stay as long as you like. Where's Casper gone, by the way?"

Molly pointed towards the ceiling.

"Upstairs with Carlos and Teddy. I don't think he gets the concept of three being a crowd."

Jeremy laughed.

"Well, I don't think they'll mind too much this time. After all, if it hadn't been for Casper..."

Teddy's father shuddered slightly.

"I know. It hardly bears thinking about. Perhaps the Casper Beaumont International Detective Agency has a future after all."

"You have to admit, it was pretty good detective work."

Jonathon nodded.

"It was. As soon as we realised that Teddy wasn't with Carlos and that there was something wrong, we called the police. Then, Casper got his phone out and started googling. I was actually going to tell him off for not taking things seriously. But he'd put in the name of the factory in the shot that Teddy had sent him of the disused railway, and up it came. Even the police were impressed. The reasoning was, given that she had sent it yesterday, there was every possibility that she was still somewhere in the vicinity. We drove straight there."

"It was good of your wife to ring and tell us what was happening." Jeremy laughed suddenly. "I don't think I've ever seen Carlos move so quickly."

"I must admit," said Jonathon, his expression suddenly darkening. "When I saw the area I started to fear the worst."

"It is pretty isolated over there," agreed Jeremy. "I took a walk down there once when a train had been cancelled and I had a load of time to kill. I don't think I saw another soul. I guess if you wanted to get up to no good, that would be the kind of place to do it."

Aubrey, who was slumped on Jeremy's lap, agreed. The yard and its surroundings was exactly the kind of place where bad things might happen. It was the kind of place where you could scream and struggle as much as you liked, nobody would hear you. He tucked his tail more tightly into himself. He didn't think that he would ever forget Teddy's face when the locksmith had finally pulled the door open. She wasn't a big girl but she had seemed even smaller as she had emerged, white-faced and blinking, her hair tousled. She had run straight to her father and flung her arms around his waist, burying her head into his chest, before noticing Carlos who had been standing patiently to one side. She had looked at him uncertainly. Almost, thought Aubrey, as though she didn't quite recognise him and the hurt in his eyes had been unmistakable. Silently she had pulled her phone from her pocket, waited for it to ping back to life, and handed it to him. He had watched as Carlos slowly read the message and then gave the phone back to her.

"Not me," he had said. "Not me."

"What did they say at the police station?" asked Jeremy. "Do they have any idea who did this?"

Jonathon shook his head.

"Not at this stage. All that's known is that it was sent from the phone that Carlos lost, which was why Teddy trusted it. But where that phone is and who's got it, they don't yet know. One of the officers there, a nice young chap in a rather smart suit, had an idea that it might somehow be connected to the anonymous letters that have been sent. Teddy told me about them," he added.

Jeremy looked thoughtful. "Why would he think that?"

"I guess because they're both unusual happenings. He was telling me that crime in this area is usually restricted to shoplifting, traffic offences, and the occasional burglary. The last real crimes of any note were when some elderly people were murdered, which was a few years ago now. Before his time, anyway. You probably remember it. I think you lived here then..."

Jonathon stumbled to a halt. He had, Aubrey thought, just recalled that Carlos's mother, although not elderly, had been one of the victims.

Jeremy gave a rueful half-smile.

"Yes, I remember it. We all do."

And so they did, thought Aubrey. They had, all of them, himself included, been in the thick of it.

Jonathon cleared his throat and then continued.

"Anyway, since that time, apparently it's been all quiet on the western front so to speak. To now have an outbreak of poison pen letters and a kidnap occur at the same time is nothing short of astonishing. One of them alone would be remarkable."

"The letters seem to have stopped for the time being," said Jeremy. "As far as I'm aware. I guess that more people might have received them, but I don't think that anybody has come forward. Did the officer have any idea what the connection between them and Teddy's kidnap might be?"

"I think he thought that it was a bit of a coincidence that Carlos had received one of the letters and that, after he lost his phone, it was then used to trap Teddy. He did think that perhaps..." he paused and hesitated before continuing. "He did think that somehow Carlos might be central to all this. He told me about the incident at the railway station," he added.

Jeremy shifted slightly in his chair. Aubrey could tell he felt uncomfortable and he understood why. He felt the same. Both he and Jeremy had always been protective of Carlos. So was Vincent, in his own Vincent type way. As if Carlos hadn't had enough to deal with in his short life, the thought that someone was now somehow spinning some kind of malicious web around him would hardly bear thinking about.

"But if this is about Carlos, why were all the other letters sent?" asked Molly. "I had one too, you know."

Jonathon frowned.

"I don't know. Maybe a kind of smoke screen? You know what they say about hiding a tree."

Aubrey looked up, interested. No, what did they say about hiding a tree?

Molly smiled.

"Yes, in a forest."

Aubrey tucked his head under Jeremy's arm. Who wanted to hide a tree anyway?

"But why? To what purpose?" asked Jeremy.

"I can't imagine." Jonathon cleared his throat slightly. "I

don't suppose, I mean... has Carlos got any enemies do you think? I mean, has he upset someone or anything like that? Maybe someone at work?"

Molly shook her head. "I don't think so." She turned to Jeremy. "Has he?"

"Not that I'm aware of. If he had, I'm sure he would have told us."

Aubrey suddenly felt even more uncomfortable. Why would anybody not like Carlos? He was as open and decent as the day was long. And it was true what Jeremy had said, if Carlos had a problem or was worried about something he always told them even if it was later rather than sooner. But apart from being upset when he had received those letters, he just seemed his usual self. Well, up until the point when Teddy had disappeared, anyway. He raised his head as Teddy, Carlos and Casper came into the room. Jonathon Beaumont stood up.

"Come on then, you two. We ought to get going. Your mother will be wondering where we are."

CHAPTER THIRTY-SIX

Jeremy thought again about the letter that Molly had been sent. Her mentioning it when Jonathon Beaumont had been with them had brought it back with force, although in truth it had never been too far below the surface. The letter had been particularly horrible and had left little to the imagination when it came to detail. It was all very well people saying that such things should be ignored, that the problem was with the writer and not the receiver, but it was difficult. The words stuck and they hurt, as they were intended to. He suddenly remembered something that his granny used to say, something about sticks and stones breaking bones but words could never hurt you. Well, it wasn't true. Bones can mend but words were poisoned arrows that found their target, and then quivered and stuck.

He sighed and got up from behind his desk. Today was going to be another difficult day. Apart from the prospect of another governor's meeting with the appalling Gerald Crawley in attendance, he still hadn't found a replacement for Rissa. Some of the kids had begun to take advantage of the situation by bunking off, just when he'd actually started to see an improvement in attendance figures. Those that weren't skiving were running rings around the various supply teachers he'd managed to get hold of. It was in danger of becoming a school sport. And then there was this flu thing that seemed to be going around. Three members of staff had rung in sick already this morning, which meant even fewer teachers on the ground. It wasn't like a college where you could just cancel classes or send students home. Here he was dealing with under sixteens and one way or another he had to keep them contained on the premises.

He walked over to the window and stared out. The faint wisps rising from behind the gym wall told him that the smokers were engaging in their favourite pastime. He could, he supposed, go out there and creep up on them, but then what? They could detect a teacher a mile off, it was a kind of inbuilt radar. They would have scattered before he got anywhere near them. Anyway, even if he did manage to catch them, they were like a secret cell. They would simply go underground and find somewhere else to smoke. At least this way he knew where they were and at least they were still on the school premises. Really, he needed to find another way to tackle it. Nicotine was, he had read, one of the most addictive of substances and one of the hardest to give up, but that didn't mean that those kids out there were a lost cause.

It had been Rissa who had suggested that they should invite some kind of health worker in to talk to the kids at assembly about the dangers of smoking, preferably with some horrendous visuals of diseased and damaged organs to terrify the bejesus out of them, but after she had died it somehow dropped off the agenda along with most of her other ideas. Those kind of initiatives needed someone behind them to focus and drive them through, and nobody else on the staff had seemed either willing or able to pick up where she had left off.

Much as he would have like to do it himself, he simply didn't have the time.

The image of Rissa's bright, interested face danced before him and he felt suddenly depressed. It wasn't just that he still hadn't found anybody to replace her on a permanent basis, it was much more than that. Apart from the fact that her death had been such a waste of a promising young life, she had been a real breath of fresh air. She had been exactly the type of teacher that Sir Franks needed. In fact, exactly the kind of teacher that all schools needed. All right, it was true that some of her ideas were a bit off the wall, and certainly not all of them would have been workable, but at least she had ideas which was more than could be said for some of the other staff.

The clock on the wall showed that it was nearly lunchtime. He had promised himself when he took office that he wouldn't spend all his time behind his desk. In addition to regularly walking the corridors and undertaking break duty when he could, he made a point of eating in the school refectory with the pupils at least once a week. It was part of his drive to involve himself properly in the life of the school, and he'd planned to have his lunch in there today. But his experience to date of the menu provided by Sir Franks had been pretty depressing and improving it was yet another challenge to add to his ever-growing list.

While his own memory of school dinners could hardly be called inspiring, at least the food had been recognisable and cooked by proper school cooks. The food served at Sir Franks provided fuel, but that was about all it did. It could hardly be called healthy, unless you counted an invariable diet of reconstituted breaded chicken and re-heated cardboard thin frozen pizzas healthy. Even those that brought in their own lunch often didn't fare much better. He'd once looked in the so-called lunch boxes of some Year Eight pupils when searching for contraband. At least three of them had contained nothing more than a solitary packet of crisps.

He ran his hand across his forehead. It felt stuffy in here. He needed to get out, go for a walk, get away from these four walls. He didn't think that he could face the ultra-processed crap that would undoubtedly be on offer in the school refectory today.

Alfonso's was packed. The clatter of crockery and cutlery against the backdrop of the lunchtime diners was cheerful compared to the solitary atmosphere of his office and he was glad that he'd decided to come out. It would be the pick-me-up he needed for the rest of the day and, while Alfonso's menu might not be extensive, at least it contained fresh ingredients and was cooked on the premises.

Alfonso had waved at him as he came in, which had cheered him still further. There was nothing like a smiling welcome to lift the mood. He was glad to see that Alfonso was looking a lot more like his old self. His face had lost that haunted look and he was chatting away to customers as he served them, just as he had before. Hopefully he was feeling a little better about the poison pen letters, especially as he now knew that he hadn't been the only one to receive them.

He picked up the menu and ran his eye over it, although he didn't need to. He ate in here often enough to know it by heart and he'd already decided before he came in that he'd have one of Alfonso's special toasted cheese paninis followed by a good hefty slice of whatever the cake of the day was. That should set him up for the afternoon. In any event, a bite of Alfonso's tablecloth would be more palatable than any of the shite being served up in the school dining room today.

He put the menu back down and glanced around him. In

the far corner sat a man with his back to him. He couldn't see his face but there was something faintly familiar about him, something about the set of his shoulders, and for the moment he couldn't think what. As he watched, a thin-faced woman pushed open the café door and made her way over to him. The man stood up and, leaning towards her, muttered something in her ear, which made her smile.

Jeremy didn't know why he thought so but there seemed to be something clandestine about the couple. They didn't look like man and wife, that was for sure. There was something too intimate about them for that. He smiled to himself. What a sad indictment that if a couple appeared affectionate in public then the inference was that they weren't married. But it was true. He couldn't remember the last time he had openly shown any display of affection to Molly outside of the house, apart from a peck on the cheek if he met her from a train or something.

And then the man turned his head. Jeremy felt a jolt of recognition and an unwelcome snake of suspicion began to uncoil itself.

CHAPTER THIRTY-SEVEN

Jeremy poured himself another whisky, even though he'd already had one large one. Molly wouldn't be pleased. While she supported him in his work and took a real interest in the day to day life of Sir Franks, she had made it pretty clear of late that, in her opinion, it was taking too much out of him. She wasn't quite monitoring his drinking, but it would be difficult not to notice that the tougher the day, the later he went to bed and the further down the level of whisky in the bottle slipped. And today had been a particularly tough day. The incipient headache that had threatened earlier ratcheted up a notch. He sipped at his drink, aware of the dull throbbing in his head and the slight needling ache that was developing in his right ear.

There were some difficult pupils at Sir Franks, God alone knew, but Milo Russel was a case apart. Something that he had sincerely hoped to avoid when he took up post, he was now being forced to seriously consider. Excluding a pupil was the absolute last resort and if he did it, he had to be sure that he was right. It should, he knew, only be considered in situations where pupil behaviour couldn't be remedied within the school.

However he looked at it, Milo Russel's propensity to dissolve into sudden unpredictable screaming rages in the middle of lessons couldn't be remedied within the school. It was disturbing and upsetting, and it stopped the other pupils learning. There was no point in ordering him out of the room, he simply refused to go. And anyway, even if they did somehow manage to manhandle him outside of the classroom, short of shoving him into a lockable cupboard, they had nowhere suitable to put him. The latest incident, this afternoon, had taken place during a history lesson and had resulted in the history teacher taking the other children out while the rage burned itself to a cinder. Several of the pupils had then refused to re-enter, claiming to be frightened. And in truth, they probably were.

Not for the first time, he had checked Milo's file. The boy came from what would generally be considered to be a 'good' family. He had two older brothers, both of whom had attended Sir Franks and neither of whom had ever given any trouble. He knew from staffroom chatter that his mother was a stalwart of the Women's Institute and his father was a popular leader at the local youth club. On the face of it there was nothing amiss. After the last incident, he had called Milo's parents in to discuss the problem. They had expressed complete surprise, adamant that they had seen nothing of this kind of behaviour. But in spite of their protestations, in his heart of hearts, Jeremy knew instinctively that something was wrong inside the boy's home. The father had been a little too vociferous in his denial of Milo's behaviour and the mother a little too willing to follow her husband's line. Jeremy hadn't missed the quick nervous sideways glance she had given him before speaking.

The fact was that teenagers, for all their rampant hormones and extremes of emotion, didn't just fly into furious rages at the slightest provocation. It was ironic really that Carlos, who most definitely could not be said to have come from a good home and had suffered what could only be called a distinctly disadvantaged start in life, had never given them a moment's concern with regard to his behaviour since he had come to live with them. The worst thing he had done was to arrive home inebriated after drinking cider in the park with some of his friends, and even then he had been what Jeremy would describe as a jolly drunk. He had simply staggered in, told them a joke which he couldn't remember the end of, and then crashed in a drunken heap on the sofa.

He felt the pain in his head thicken and an irritating tickle start at the back of his throat. He soothed it away with another gulp of whisky and thought about Milo again. If he did suspend him this time, and he knew that really he had little choice, he would in effect be abandoning him in the very place he suspected his problems lay – his home. It was only a suspicion, albeit one based on experience, but he knew very well how easily witch hunts were started and if they were unfounded, the traumatising effects could last for years. But be that as it may, and even though he had no evidence as such, he had a duty to report it to the relevant authority. Gone were the days when teachers and other professionals could simply turn a blind eye. Milo clearly needed some kind of help and the school was just not equipped to deal with it.

Of course, the final decision would be his to make, but he would have to report it to the governors. And whichever way he decided to play it, Gerald Crawley would oppose it. The issue of Milo's behaviour had been raised once before and for some reason Crawley had decided to champion him. Not, Jeremy strongly suspected, because he felt any affinity with the lad. As far as he was aware, he didn't even know him. No, it was just another opportunity to undermine his headship. According to Crawley, who had never been witness to the tsunami of one of

Milo's classroom rages, it was simply teenage behaviour which the school should be more than capable of dealing with. He had looked round the room for support as he said it, and several of the more craven governors had nodded along with him.

He reached for the box of tissues standing on the little side table and blew his nose. At the thought of the governors his spirits sank a little further. It had been a particularly trying meeting today, and he hadn't even raised the issue of Milo Russel. Gerald Crawley had surpassed himself in managing to be more obnoxious than usual, and it had infected every item on the agenda. He had arrived early and bustled in with his usual air of bumptious self-importance, as if Jeremy should be grateful that he was granting him some time from his very busy schedule, like he was head of NATO or something, and then seated himself squarely in the middle of the table. With an unnecessary flourish, he had fanned his papers out across the surface, thereby ensuring that he took more than his fair share of space. After which, everything had gone downhill. Every idea or suggestion that had been made, he had shot down, leaping in before the person had finished speaking. The man practically exuded a kind of triumphant negativity and the most annoying thing was that he looked positively pleased with himself every time he scored what he undoubtedly considered to be a point. Jeremy had never considered himself to be a violent man, but there were occasions when he thought that it might be very satisfying to throttle someone with his bare hands.

He looked up as Aubrey nudged his way round the door and walked towards him, tail in the air.

"Evening, Aubrey." Jeremy raised his glass in greeting. "What shall we do about Gerald Crawley?"

Kill him, thought Aubrey. He didn't actually know the man, never having met him, but he'd listened to Jeremy telling Molly and Carlos about him over dinner. From what Aubrey could tell, this Gerald Crawley sounded like a human version of Piranesi, the posh cat up the road who was forever telling the rest of the cats what to do and how to do it. There was no feline task on this earth that Piranesi was not an expert on. From ratting to tree climbing, Piranesi had it nailed. As Vincent had said, it wouldn't be so bad if he didn't know for a fact that Piranesi slept on a big silk cushion and had his food cut up for him by his owner. He never lifted a paw for himself. He could hardly be called a cat of the people.

Aubrey jumped onto Jeremy's lap and started to settle himself just as Jeremy's mobile began to ring. One ear pricked, he listened as Jeremy began talking. Something was going down, it was obvious. The air around them felt suddenly charged and from being slumped in the chair with tiredness, Jeremy had now sat up with a sort of pleased, excited look on his face. They both turned as Molly came in, her expression stern.

"Jeremy, if that's work..."

"It's not," he interrupted her, finishing his call and putting his phone away again. "Well, it is in a way."

Molly sat down and leaned forward, a slight frown creasing her forehead.

"Either it is or it isn't."

"It was that police officer I told you about. DC Renshaw, Rench. The one in the suit. He promised me that he'd update me if they found anything. Well, they think they've got the writer of at least one of the poison pen letters." He paused for a moment and drew breath. "It's Gerald Crawley."

"Goodness."

Aubrey watched as Molly slowly absorbed this information.

"Did he say which letter?" she asked at last.

"Not yours," said Jeremy quickly, reading her thoughts. "It was the one that went to the girl at the town hall. Ava, I think her name is. He used his work computer to write it and somebody found it."

"How?" asked Molly. "Did they hack it or something?"

Jeremy shook his head.

"No, they didn't need to. At the town hall they have what they call an OT department. Instead of an IT department," he added.

"A what?"

"An OT department, it stands for Open Technology. Apparently it means that any employee can use any machine. The line is that office technology should only be used for office business, therefore there should be no issue with all computers being available to all employees." Jeremy paused and grinned. "Bet it doesn't apply to the Chief Exec."

Molly laughed.

"I bet it doesn't. So how does it actually work?"

"Well, open technology extends to open desks, so in theory at any point any employee could sit at any desk. They don't, of course. Being territorial like all humans, they have their own computers on their own desks along with their pot plants and family photographs. But that's the theory. Anyway, Crawley was off sick one day and somebody else in that office was having trouble with their own computer so logged on to his. But not before noting that Crawley hadn't password-protected it. Not being exactly popular with his fellow employees, this bloke decided to have a quick trawl round Crawley's documents before getting on with his own work. And there it was. In a file marked Important Correspondence."

"And he read it?"

Jeremy nodded.

"Of course. I mean, you'd have to. A file marked Importance Correspondence is just asking to be opened."

Sometimes, thought Aubrey, you could almost believe that Jeremy was a cat.

"So what happened?" asked Molly. "Did he report it?"

"Yes. Even if this bloke had liked Crawley, which he didn't, it wasn't the kind of thing that could be ignored. It was really nasty. And practically everybody in the building knew that Ava had received it. She didn't hold back in telling people. If you remember, she more or less went straight to the police."

"You'd have to be pretty stupid to do that kind of thing at work though," said Molly.

"Or arrogant. He's some kind of manager, so presumably it never occurred to him that anybody else would actually have the temerity to touch his computer, let alone open any of his documents. I mean, really, you have to laugh. Typical of Crawley. Thinks he's so clever." He looked thoughtful for a moment. "Do you know, Moll, I always thought there was something a bit different about the letter that Ava received. Do you remember, DC Renshaw showed it to me? There was something a bit more unhinged about it."

Molly gave a small laugh.

"Well none of the letters were what you might call rational."

"That's true. But the others seemed a bit more, I don't know, calculated. A bit studied somehow. Crafted I suppose you'd call it."

"So they didn't find any of the other letters?"

Jeremy shook his head.

"No. Just that one. But the police went to his home and took his laptop. They've also got his mobile."

"Did they find anything?"

"They did. They found what DC Renshaw described as some interesting material. But it makes me think, if Crawley didn't write the other letters, what gave him the idea to write Ava's?"

"Perhaps he overheard something?"

"Maybe. Although I've just remembered, Chloe Kennedy told me that when she received her first letter she told her manager about it. What's the betting that Gerald Crawley is her manager?"

"It's easy enough to check," said Molly. "Text Chloe and ask her."

"I will. I'll do it in the morning." He hesitated and then continued. "Moll, there's something else..."

"What?"

"I saw something today. When I was in Alfonso's. I mean, it's probably my imagination working overtime but..."

He stopped mid-sentence and started a loud hacking cough. Molly stood up and placed her hand lightly on his forehead.

"I think you ought to be in bed. Come on, you can bring your whisky with you and tell me about it there."

CHAPTER THIRTY-EIGHT

Jeremy sat up slightly and pulled his pillow more comfortably behind his head. He stared glumly at the wall opposite. He was supposed to be running assembly this morning. Would it have been cancelled or would somebody else have picked it up? It would be a shame if it hadn't gone ahead. A group of Year Nines were scheduled to host it today and, having learned from experience to insist that content must be submitted to him for approval first, he knew what a lot of work they had put into it.

And then there was Milo Russel. He needed to start the process of suspension sooner rather than later, it couldn't just be left indefinitely. They'd been lucky so far, the boy hadn't actually harmed anybody. At least not physically. But the potential was there.

His felt his thoughts scattering like grapeshot, each one rolling away before he could grasp it. There were what seemed like a hundred and one things to deal with. Would his secretary remember to cancel his meeting with the health and safety inspector today? Had anybody else phoned in sick? Did the school actually have enough staff to manage? They couldn't just keep doubling up classes, but what else could they do?

He supposed that if the worst really came to the worst, the kids could be herded into the assembly hall and the gym and kept there, but putting them all together would be like cramming them into a tinder box. Excited and volatile by the change in routine, any spark could set them off. He flopped back again. It was no good worrying about it and anyway, there was nothing that he could do. Molly had confiscated his mobile.

He reached out and pulled another tissue from the box. Molly had been right to insist that he stay in bed today. No matter how much he had to do, he was in no state to do it. When he'd woken this morning, he'd hardly been able to put one foot in front of another and, dosed up as he was with cold and flu remedies, his thoughts had taken on a distinctly fuzzy edge. But hopefully this virus or whatever it was would burn itself out within a day, or two days at the most. It would have to, he couldn't afford the time out. He reached his hand across the bed and stroked Aubrey who was laid out on his back next to him.

"What do you think, Aubrey? Will they have cancelled the assembly?"

Aubrey opened one eye slightly and then shut it again. He didn't know what an assembly was and he didn't care. He was sorry that Jeremy was feeling so rough but he couldn't deny that he was having a great day himself. The only time that he was legitimately allowed on the beds was when they were occupied by somebody who was ill. Any other time he would be chucked off as soon as he was spotted. At least by Molly and Jeremy. Carlos had a rather more liberal attitude. He stretched and flexed his claws. Since Teddy had been found, things seemed to have settled down again, for which he was grateful. In common with many cats, one of the things that he valued most was routine. He gave a small purr as Jeremy tickled his ears, and then drifted off to sleep again.

Jeremy looked down at him and felt a swell of affection. He was a dear old cat. Warm and loving he always seemed to be around when he was needed. It could have been very different, he knew. When you went to a rescue centre you didn't know what you were going to get, but with Aubrey there was no doubt that they'd struck lucky. And there was another sunny spot on the horizon too. Crawley would have to vacate his post as a governor now. If Crawley didn't offer his resignation and he wouldn't put it past him to try and bluff it out, as head teacher, he was now surely in a position to demand it. Rench had indicated very firmly that the police would pursue a charge against him, in which case there would be no place for him at Sir Franks. Or indeed anywhere else. It was unlikely that he would be able to keep his job, especially as the recipient of his letter was a fellow employee.

As one of his more irritating ex-colleagues used to say, what goes around comes around, and in this case it had the ring of truth. If Crawley had been a less unpleasant person then probably whoever had uncovered the letter wouldn't have gone looking in his files. And it was true what he'd surmised the previous evening, Chloe had confirmed by text this morning that Crawley was indeed her manager. Jeremy smiled to himself. While not a vindictive man, he would have given a great deal to be the proverbial fly on the wall when the police had knocked at Crawley's door. What, he wondered, had been the other stuff that the police had found on his computer?

At the thought of the police his mind turned again to his suspicions of yesterday. Should he tell them? Molly had made it clear that she thought he should, her argument being that it was better to err on the side of caution, and she had a point. But what if he was completely wrong? After all, it was only a suspicion, he had nothing concrete to go on. And if he was wrong he could be opening up a positive shit show on a perfectly innocent man. But the more he thought about it, the more the pieces seemed to fall into place...

He turned his head as the door opened and Molly came in.

"Here," she said, passing him his iPad, "I thought you might like this. I've downloaded the apps for you."

Jeremy took the iPad, looked down at the screen and then looked up again.

"Thanks, Moll, but I don't think I'm up to playing any games yet."

"Not games," said Molly patiently. "Television. I thought you might like to watch some TV to pass the time. But," she paused and looked back on her way out. "No emailing."

Jeremy smiled and tapped on the screen. There was no denying, modern technology was amazing. He'd been brought up in an era when households generally had only one television and that set had a limited amount of programmes to watch. Nowadays you could watch hundreds of channels on almost any device, including a phone, and Carlos had told him that you could even view it on a watch although he couldn't see the point of that.

"What do you reckon, Aubrey? What do you fancy watching?"

Cats, thought Aubrey. Or dogs. Don't mind which. He lifted his head and watched with interest as Jeremy scrolled the screen.

"What about some true crime?" asked Jeremy. "Some juicy Edwardian murder?"

Aubrey lowered his head again. Only if it's got cats in it, he thought. He closed his eyes and curled himself in against

Jeremy, luxuriating in the closeness. He jumped as Jeremy suddenly sat up straight, and shoved the iPad under his nose.

"Oh my God. Aubrey, look…"

Aubrey looked. He couldn't see what the fuss was about. Just some woman in a bath.

CHAPTER THIRTY-NINE

Jeremy dropped the iPad on the duvet and looked up as the bedroom door opened again.

"Visitor for you," said Molly. "DC Renshaw."

DC Renshaw, elegantly attired as always, advanced into the room.

"Rench, please." He smiled at Jeremy. "Mrs Goodman answered your mobile when I called and told me that you were ill. I thought I'd pop round, if you're feeling up to it."

Molly turned back towards the door.

"I'll leave you two to it. Give me a shout if you need anything. I'll bring some coffee up in a bit."

Jeremy smiled in greeting.

"Come on in. Drag up a chair," he said, indicating the small upholstered chair in the corner of the room.

Rench carried the chair over and sat down. He leaned forward, his clasped hands swinging loosely between his knees.

"I thought you might want the latest update."

"Is it about the interesting stuff that you found on Gerald Crawley's computer?"

"Well, yes." Rench hesitated and then continued. "I can't see any harm in telling you, especially as he's one of your school governors, so it could be said that you have a legitimate interest, but I would prefer it if this didn't go any further."

"Of course," said Jeremy, fighting back the urge to start coughing again.

"As you know," continued Rench. "We had a warrant to search Crawley's house and we discovered that he has two laptops. The first one was in the room he uses as a study and there was nothing of any interest on that. But something at the back of my neck told me to keep looking, so we did. We'd almost given up, when his wife came into the room. She didn't say anything, but she kept looking out of the window, and then back at us. I asked her if there was anything that she wanted us to know and she shook her head. And then she looked out of the window again." He paused and smiled. "It was in the garden, in a sort of workshop that he's got out there. It was tucked up high on a shelf among some old tools. And with it there was a phone."

Jeremy looked at him. He knew what was coming next. It was a sweeping generalisation but innocent people didn't usually hide laptops or phones.

"He didn't have a password on either of them but it wouldn't have mattered if he had," continued Rench. "We'd have simply taken them away for our IT lads to look at. We didn't find any more letters, but on both devices there were files marked Summer Camp. It seems that Crawley accompanied the local youth club on some of their camping trips. And, along with several other men, indulged his penchant for home movies. But not the sort that you'd show at a family party."

Jeremy felt his stomach spiral downwards. It was even worse than he'd suspected. The local youth centre was where

Milo Russel's father was a leader. He felt suddenly unutterably depressed. So it looked as though he might have been right. Of course, if Milo Russel's father was one of these other men, his penchant for teenaged boys didn't mean that he had abused his own son. But he'd read of cases where just one child of the family was singled out for abuse, and something had to be the explanation for Milo's behaviour. Not for the first time, he thought about the dreadful outward ripple effect of abuse and the sheer utter bloody selfishness of the abusers. It damaged victims for years and infected their lives at almost every level. He cleared his throat.

"So where was Crawley when you were searching?" he asked at last.

"In his kitchen pretending to read the newspaper. He tried to stop us going into the garden, naturally. He started blustering on about how we'd invaded his privacy long enough and that he numbered several senior police officers among his personal friends."

Jeremy laughed.

"I doubt Crawley could number anybody among his friends, personal or otherwise."

"Anyway, we obviously ignored him."

"What was Crawley's reaction when you found the stuff?" he asked.

DC Renshaw gave a wry smile.

"As you might expect. At first he tried to pretend that he didn't know anything about it, said that it was an old laptop and somebody else must have used it. He claimed that he didn't even know it was in the shed. It all came a bit unstuck when we pointed out that he was one of the people in the videos."

"What will happen to them?" asked Jeremy.

"Well, given that the boys in the videos are clearly

underage, and given also that the adults were in a position of trust, I should think that they'll be looking at a custodial sentence. And with Crawley there's the letter to take into consideration as well."

"Why do you think he wrote it?"

Rench shrugged.

"Sheer bloody nastiness, I suspect. By all accounts, young Ava is a popular girl. I think that he probably just resented her and wanted to bring her down a peg or two."

"That sounds about right," Jeremy agreed. He hesitated and then continued. "About the other letters..."

"What about them?"

"I saw something yesterday. I wasn't sure whether to tell you about it or not. It's only a suspicion. I could be entirely wrong, but I've been thinking about it..."

Rench tipped his head to one side and looked at Jeremy, a curious expression on his face.

"What was it that you saw?"

"I was in Alfonso's. I'd decided to have lunch there and was just looking at the menu when a woman came in."

"Yes?"

"She went up to a man sitting in the corner and there was something about them. They looked, well, like a couple, if you know what I mean. And then the man turned round."

Rench gave a small smile, as if, thought Aubrey, he had already anticipated Jeremy's answer.

"It was Dean Ingram," said Jeremy.

"And what is it that you suspected?" asked Rench.

Jeremy ran his hand across his forehead.

"It was weird. It was like one of those kaleidoscope things that we had as kids, do you remember them? No, you're probably too young, but it was like lots of pieces suddenly fell into place and made a complete picture."

Rench remained silent and waited for Jeremy to continue.

"At first I didn't want to believe it, but the more I thought about it the more of a possibility it seemed." He hesitated and then continued. "Something that Teddy's father said came back to me. He said that the letters may have been a smoke screen for something else and that the best place to hide a tree was in a forest. I sort of dismissed it at the time because he thought that the letters might have been about something to do with Carlos. But when I was sitting in Alfonso's, I suddenly realised. It was all about Rissa. She had money. Lots of money. Which, as her husband, he would inherit unless she'd made a will to the contrary which I assume she hadn't, on the basis that most young people don't. But even if she had, it would have been invalidated on her marriage. And I think that he knew he had to act sooner rather than later because her plan was to eventually give her money away to a good cause."

Rench tipped his head to one side.

"So what do you think happened?"

"I think that Dean Ingram set it all up. They got married not long after they met, you know? Ingram told me that himself. He presented it as a sort of love at first sight thing. She was quite an open person and my guess is that she told him all about herself, including the fact that she was loaded and that she had at one time suffered from fainting fits. I think he saw it as a golden opportunity, but I couldn't quite work out how he'd done it. Then, just before you came in, I was watching a television programme. It was one of those true crime things and it was showing the story of George Joseph Smith, the Brides in the Bath case."

For a moment Jeremy fell silent.

"You think I'm being a twat, don't you?" he said at last.

"No. I know about George Joseph Smith. He married wealthy women who very soon afterwards conveniently drowned in their bath. He tipped them up by their ankles. And in this case, if she's already been fed alcohol and sleeping pills it wouldn't take much." Rench smiled suddenly. "To quote the lads at the nick, I've done all the courses."

Jeremy breathed a slow sigh of relief and continued.

"If you remember, the letter that Rissa received was produced at the inquest and Ingram gave evidence that Rissa had suffered quite serious mental health problems in the past, which seemed to explain what had happened. Her parents denied that she had ever had any such problem though. I thought at the time that they were just being protective. I'm not so sure now."

They both turned as Molly came in bearing a tray. She set it down on the bedside cabinet and looked at them.

"You two look very serious."

"I was just telling Rench the stuff I was talking to you about last night." He paused for a moment. "You were here before me on this one, weren't you?" he asked, turning to Rench.

Rench nodded.

"I asked the chief executive at the town hall for a list of staff. He was a bit reluctant at first but, as I pointed out, it's not exactly a state secret. Anyway, he gave it to me and although there were several hundred names on it, at least it was better than nothing. And as it turned out, it was indeed a lot better than nothing."

"You mean..."

"I do. Dean Ingram works at the town hall in the Finance Department. I should say, he did work there. Apparently he's resigned. But clearly it was easy for him to get the letters to the right people. The irony is that the one letter he wanted to deliver was the easiest of the lot. He just put it in her bag after she died."

"Knowing that somebody would collect it. Or, if they didn't, he could simply take the bag into school. Christ. But why didn't he send the letter while she was alive?"

"I think it was because she would probably have reported it to us. The accusations were so far from the truth that there was every possibility that, far from being upset, she would have seen it for what it was, a piece of gratuitous spite. All that stuff about her mental state and so on would have been far less convincing."

Jeremy nodded.

"I think you're right. So what put you on to him?"

Rench gave a small smile.

"When a person, especially a young person, and especially a young rich person, dies unexpectedly, it does rather make one wonder who benefits."

"He didn't try to hide the fact that she had money though. I mean, he told me himself that she was loaded," said Jeremy.

"Because he knew that at some point it would come out. There was no point in hiding it. In fact, it would have looked more suspect if he hadn't been open about it."

"That's true," Jeremy looked thoughtful. "The piece about her in the local paper talked about her wanting to establish a charity. So why do you think he asked me to go to the inquest with him? I mean, surely, he would have wanted to keep it as low-profile as possible?"

"I think that he wanted to get you on side. The details of the coroner's finding would be made public anyway and if you were seen to be supportive of him it would deflect any suspicion away from him. Anyway, I decided to dig around a bit and see what I could find out about him."

Jeremy leaned forward.

"And?"

"Initially there wasn't much. He seemed an ordinary sort of

bloke doing an ordinary sort of job. His father died from a heart attack, His mother was suffering from Alzheimer's and died shortly after. Interestingly, how do you think his mother died?"

Jeremy caught his breath.

"How?"

"She fainted in the bath and drowned."

CHAPTER FORTY

J eremy watched from the window as the kids streamed out of the gates, pushing and shoving at one another in their haste to exit. Thank goodness the flu epidemic or whatever it was had died down and they were getting the school back to some semblance of normality. Or what passed for normality at Sir Franks. He turned back and lifted his coat from the old-fashioned coat stand in the corner of the room. All the paperwork that was stacking up could wait. It would still be there tomorrow.

He smiled suddenly at the memory of a fairy story that he had been told when he was about five. It was something to do with elves, he thought. Elves who had helped someone out who was overworked. They had crept in at night and completed all his work for him. Wouldn't it be great, he thought, if the elves got into his office tonight and cleared his desk? He wasn't sure what they'd make of the preparations for the next Ofsted, but no doubt they'd cope.

He shrugged his arms into his coat and made his way out to the car park. The wind blew a slight chill, signalling the end of autumn sunshine and presaging the first hint of winter. He hurried towards his car. He was glad that the mystery of Jamal and the pigeonholes had been solved, Carlos had told him about it last night. It was a story as old as time – a secret romantic yearning. Jamal had discovered that it was the woman's birthday and he'd place a card in her pigeonhole. He'd confessed to him during a coffee break. According to Carlos he'd already guessed. The woman came into the refectory every day and Jamal was always giving her extra chips. In any event, hopefully that had put Carlos's mind at rest.

Settling himself into his car, he switched on the engine and turned to the radio. The newscaster's voice was low and solemn as it announced the arrest of a local man for the outbreak of poison pen letters that had been troubling the community. He turned the engine off again while he listened. He'd known it was coming, Rench had told him. After some initial difficulty persuading his boss, Rench had eventually been allowed to apply for the permission that he needed to search Ingram's house.

Unlike Gerald Crawley, Ingram had password-protected his laptop, but according to Rench they had found nothing incriminating on it anyway. Ironically, it had been Molly's letter that had tripped him up along with a letter to somebody called Harker who had never reported it. The first copies had caught in the printer and Ingram had yanked them out and thrown them in the wastepaper basket. Where they had remained.

Jeremy smiled to himself. On such little things are we caught. How often did he empty the wastepaper basket in his own study? Only when it was overflowing was the honest answer.

He switched on the engine again. Satisfying though this news was, it didn't take them any closer to identifying Ingram as a murderer. As Rench had said, they really didn't have anything to go on other than a similarity to a case in the 1900s and a strong suspicion.

The house felt warm and cosy when he let himself in. From the kitchen came the welcoming aroma of roasting chicken. He flung his coat over the banister and walked through to the sitting room. Carlos, sprawled on the rug in front of the fire and reading a catering magazine, waved a hand in greeting. On the sofa opposite him sat Rench.

Jeremy smiled.

"Hello, Rench. What are you doing here? I heard the news on the local radio by the way. Did he confess?"

Rench shook his head. "No. He went the predictable no comment route."

"But surely he hasn't got a leg to stand on?"

"He hasn't. But that doesn't stop him exercising his right to silence. He's been released on bail, which we expected. But there's more. I thought I'd drop in on my way home and tell you."

Jeremy caught his breath. "About Rissa?"

Rench nodded.

"I was curious about that woman that you saw Ingram with in Alfonso's, so I decided to check her out. Unknown to his customers, since receiving his poison pen letters, Alfonso installed some discreet cameras in the café so that he got a record of who comes and goes. On that particular day, there's clear footage of the woman and Ingram sitting together. It crossed my mind that she might have driven there and, if she had, she would probably park her car in the nearest car park. The public part of the one attached to the town hall."

"And did she?" asked Carlos.

"She did."

"How do you know?" asked Jeremy.

"Cameras again. Remember that car park is also used for the Crown Court and they're part of their security. The footage clearly shows her parking her car. By zooming in, it also showed the registration number."

Carlos dropped his magazine and turned to Jeremy, his face alight.

"I've changed my mind about being a chef. I'm going to be a detective."

Jeremy laughed.

"You could be a chef detective." He turned back to Rench. "So what happened next?"

"I thought I'd call round for a little chat."

"Did she know you were coming?" asked Carlos.

"No. And to be honest, she could have just slammed the door in my face. But she didn't."

"What did she say?"

"Well, she knew that Ingram had been arrested for the poison pen letters and she thought that was what we'd come about. So, first of all, she said that she didn't know anything about it, and that it was nothing to do with her. When I suggested that Ingram might have done considerably worse than write some nasty letters, she became a bit wary. When I pushed her she started to sing like a canary. She admitted that Ingram had told her what he'd done to his wife, but then she said that she'd thought it was just some kind of fantasy thing. She said that she didn't really take much notice of it."

"Honestly?" asked Jeremy incredulously. "Your lover tells you that he's killed his wife and you don't take much notice of it?"

"Apparently not. But I believe her when she says that she

had nothing to do with it. The problem is," Rench looked suddenly weary, "it still doesn't really amount to evidence."

Carlos sat up straighter and stared at Rench.

"What? Even though she's told you he admitted it to her?"

"It's just words, Carlos," said Jeremy. "She might have any number of reasons for saying what she did." He turned to Rench. "What about the attack on Carlos and the kidnap of Teddy?"

"Well, we found no sign of Carlos's phone but we did find a railway ticket in a coat pocket, which at least places Ingram as having taken a railway journey on the day that Carlos was attacked. With regard to the container, the owner gave us a name but it appears to be a false one. However, now Ingram has been arrested we've got his DNA, so we'll run it against the DNA found in the container. On the positive side, it gives us the possibility of a few more charges to stick on him. On the less positive side, it doesn't take us any closer to proving he's a murderer."

Jeremy's face fell.

"So is that it then?"

"For the time being," said Rench. "We're going to go over his house again."

CHAPTER FORTY-ONE

He pulled on his jacket and picked up his car keys from the tray in the hall. He felt strangely numb, but he had to do this. Really, he should have done it days ago. But he'd get it over with as quickly as possible. He felt in his pocket for the matches and gave the box a little shake. Satisfied, he pulled the front door open. In front of him, one hand raised to ring the bell, stood three police officers. He scowled.

"This is beginning to look like harassment."

DC Renshaw smiled pleasantly.

"Sorry for the early call, Mr Ingram. We'd just like a quick look round."

"What for?"

Ignoring him, two of the police officers nudged gently past him and made their way up the stairs, while the third followed him back through to the sitting room and sat down. He picked up his tablet and pretended to start searching for something. They could look over his house all they liked. They wouldn't find anything because there was nothing to find.

All they had to go on was suspicion and much good that would do them. The only person aside from himself who knew what had really happened was Jeannie, and she was solid. Jeannie wouldn't let him down. He could rely on her silence, he knew. He had committed the perfect murder, and it had been even easier than he had thought it would be. The only pity was that he couldn't announce to the world at large how clever he had been.

He let his mind run through the well-worn grooves of that night. He had watched her drink her customary gin and tonic and listened, bored, as she talked about her day at school. But then she had started going on about her trust fund again and was gabbling about her stupid idea for setting up a charitable foundation. He had sat with narrowed eyes and made the decision then and there. It was all planned, everything was in place and there was no more time to waste. And it was her own fault. Why couldn't she simply live the good life?

They could travel the world, buy what they liked, be whatever they wanted to be. He'd even let her spend some of her money on charity if it would shut her up. But no, she had to give it all away. He had felt he might choke on his own resentment. Instead, he had smiled and nodded, and then gone through to the kitchen and poured large glasses of strong red wine for both of them. It had been easy to slip the crushed tablets into hers. She had been drowsy within minutes. He had offered to run her bath and then waited as she slipped into the warm foam and closed her eyes. It had been a matter of moments to pull gently on her ankles. He really was very clever.

He'd been an idiot about the wastepaper basket though, he knew that. The fact was that he'd completely forgotten the letters were in there. But it was too late to worry about it now. What was done was done. He let his thoughts slip and slide while he listened to the officers moving around upstairs. Would he go to prison for writing the letters? He supposed that he might, but he thought it was unlikely. It was a first offence, at least the first one that the police were aware of, if he just pleaded guilty when it got to court that would go in his favour too. He might get a suspended sentence, in fact he probably would. It was well known that the prisons were overcrowded. Writing a few letters wasn't the worst of crimes. He didn't care anyway. Even if he did go to prison it wouldn't be for very long. Jeannie would still be there when he got out and he was loaded now. He could go where he liked and do what he wanted. He'd won.

For several moments all was silent and then the door to the sitting room opened and the officers who had been searching upstairs came into the room. The taller of the two smiled pleasantly at him.

"I think we're about done here, Mr Ingram."

"I should think so. And make that the last time."

He was blustering, he knew, but he couldn't stop himself. He needed to keep cool or he would be in danger of letting his nerves get the better of him. He watched as all three moved towards the door and then DC Renshaw turned back to face him.

"Oh, I nearly forgot. The keys to the container please, Mr Ingram."

His mouth went dry and his heart started a long slow thump against his chest. If only he'd left the house fifteen minutes earlier. He would have been up by the abandoned railway now and his exercise books would be mere cinders floating on the breeze. He thought quickly. Could he get there before they could? He could at least stall for time.

"What container?"

"Oh come on, Ingram. We know it's yours. You might as well give them to us. We can always get them from the owner."

"I suggest that you do that then."

DC Renshaw shrugged.

"Okay. But in the meantime, I think that I'd like you to go along with my colleagues. There are a few more questions that we'd like to put to you."

Reluctantly, Dean Ingram followed them out to the police car and then sat stony-faced as they drove to the police station. It was just as depressing as the last time he'd been in there. He sat on the chair indicated and looked at the two officers who had placed themselves on the other side of the table.

"I want my solicitor."

Not that the bloke who'd turned up last time had been any good. He'd just sat there looking bored. But he knew his rights. He was entitled to a solicitor and he was going to have one. But he would just let the questions flow over him. He wasn't going to say anything and they couldn't make him. They were full of shit anyway.

He glanced out of the window and watched as DC Renshaw climbed out of a squad car. He guessed that he'd been back to the container. He didn't know why he'd been worried, he wouldn't have found anything. He could wear all the fancy suits he liked. He was still just a stupid plod.

His heart dropped as Renshaw looked up and smiled at him.

CHAPTER FORTY-TWO

The late spring sunshine sparkled through the kitchen window, throwing a gentle light on Aubrey and Vincent who sat expectantly on the kitchen floor. It was only a matter of time before Carlos cracked and fed them something. They turned their heads as the door opened and Jeremy came in. Carlos put down the vegetable knife.

"What happened?"

Jeremy smiled, a huge grin that made him look suddenly younger.

"Guilty. Unanimous. The jury took just over two hours."

"What swung it do you think?" asked Carlos.

Jeremy pulled back a chair and sat down at the kitchen table.

"The prosecution put a pretty good case together. It was touch and go at times but it was really clever. For instance, they didn't make a big deal about how his mother had died, but then they didn't need to. I mean, how likely is it that two of your loved ones should die in the same way? And that you stand to inherit from both of them? And they were able to prove that he knew about George Joseph Smith from the books on his bookshelves. And then there were the exercise books, of course."

"What did he say about them?" Carlos sounded curious. "I mean, like, he couldn't deny that he wrote them."

Jeremy laughed.

"It was pretty much as Rench predicted. Ingram claimed that it was all just fantasy for a book that he was planning to write."

"What about all those lies then, that he told at the inquest about Rissa being depressed and that? Did they say anything about that?"

Jeremy nodded.

"They did. They tracked down the cousins in Ireland who confirmed that Rissa stayed with them that summer and that there was nothing wrong with her. They also contacted nursing homes. None of them had any record of her staying with them. And of course, there was the evidence of her own parents. Then one of the fatal blows was when the jury were told about his relationship with another woman. His façade as the decent, heart-broken, grieving widower got blown to pieces. But the real clincher was the letter that Rissa received. Or, rather, didn't receive. The one that apparently made her take her own life."

"What do you mean?"

"There were no fingerprints on it. At least, not hers. Mine were there because I found it, and so were several police officers. But not Rissa's. And neither was there any of her DNA, which they were able to check against items from her home, her hair brushes and make-up and so on."

Carlos looked thoughtful.

"Which there should have been if she'd opened and read it."

"Exactly. Ingram is not nearly as clever as he thinks he is."

"So what's going to happen to him now?"

"He'll be looking at a life sentence."

"Even if they lock him up, it won't bring her back though, will it?" said Carlos. "That Rissa. It won't bring her back."

Aubrey padded across the kitchen and parked himself on Carlos's foot. He knew what Carlos was thinking. The man who had murdered his mother had been locked up and was probably still locked up for all they knew. But it didn't bring her back. She was still dead. And she always would be.

"No, Carlos," agreed Jeremy. "It won't bring her back. I'll tell you what, let's raise a glass to her. A good one."

He rose as he spoke and reached down into the wine rack that stood in the corner of the kitchen. He lifted a bottle out and waved it at Carlos.

"This one?"

Carlos smiled. "That's one of your posh bottles."

"Well, I think we agree that she was worth it."

"Who was?" asked Molly as she walked in through the back door.

"Rissa," said Jeremy. "We're going to raise a glass to her. Ingram was found guilty by the way."

"Good," said Molly. "Let's hope he goes down for a long time."

"I forgot to tell you," said Jeremy. "A group of the kids at school have asked if they can make a small memorial garden at the top of the playing fields. Apparently they want to grow vegetables in it."

"Do they?" asked Carlos, momentarily distracted as always by the mention of food. "What sort of vegetables?"

"Legal ones, I hope," said Jeremy as he poured the wine and passed the glasses to Carlos and Molly. He raised his hand.

"To Rissa."

He fell silent. Molly and Carlos hadn't known Rissa, but he had. He had seen her bright smile and heard her light laugh. He had smelt her fresh perfume and listened as she outlined her latest ideas for their pupils. She was gone, but she wouldn't be forgotten.

Carlos drained his glass and cleared his throat.

"I've been thinking. About the future and that."

"Have you? What about it?"

The astonishment in Jeremy's tone was evident. When he was the same age as Carlos he barely thought about the next day, far less that strange hinterland called the future.

"Are you worried about something?" asked Molly.

Carlos shook his head.

"No. I was thinking, like, what I might do next."

"Are you planning on leaving the town hall?" asked Jeremy. "If it's because of Ingram..."

"It's not that," said Carlos. "I like working at the town hall. I've already really learnt loads and it's good working with Jamal. But I don't want it to be forever."

Aubrey raised his head. There was no such thing as forever. Forever was just until the next thing happened. As he knew only too well.

"Blimey. It sounds like this calls for another glass." Jeremy reached for the bottle and topped up their glasses. "So what have you been thinking?"

Carlos shuffled slightly and looked uncomfortable.

"I've opened a savings account. And, like, in about five years, I want to open my own restaurant. Maybe start with something small, like a pop-up or something."

"That sounds like an excellent idea," said Molly. "Are you thinking somewhere local or further afield?"

"I was thinking maybe Brighton," said Carlos.

Aubrey, Vincent and Moses strolled across the lawn and then settled themselves quietly in a flower bed. Aubrey watched as Moses stretched out a little paw to dab at an insect that immediately scuttled away. He felt a strange melancholy. He knew why. It was all that talk about this Brighton place. He couldn't see why Carlos had to go anywhere. Why couldn't they all just stay as they were?

"You all right, Aubsie?"

He turned to face Vincent.

"Vin, how long is five years?"

Vincent shrugged.

"Dunno mate. A long time."

Aubrey suddenly felt more cheerful. Vincent was right. Five years was a long time. Anything could happen in five years.

ALSO BY ALISON O'LEARY

ACKNOWLEDGEMENTS

A massive and heartfelt thank you to John for his unfailing support and understanding. Thanks also to Jolyon for his tech support and patience.

None of the Cat Noir series would have been written had it not been for the real Aubrey, a fantastic rescue cat who never missed a food opportunity, but gave us years of love and affection. So thank you, Aubrey. Your memory lives on.

Last, as ever, thanks and appreciation to the brilliant team at Bloodhound who have been, as always, a real pleasure to work with.

ABOUT THE AUTHOR

I was born in London and spent my teenage years in Hertfordshire where I spent large amounts of time reading novels, watching daytime television and avoiding school.

Failing to gain any qualifications in science whatsoever, the dream of being a forensic scientist collided with reality when a careers teacher suggested that I might like to work in a shop. I don't think she meant Harrods.

Later studying law, I decided to teach rather than go into practice and have spent many years teaching mainly criminal law and criminology to young people and adults.

I enjoy reading crime novels, doing crosswords, and drinking wine. Not necessarily in that order.

A NOTE FROM THE PUBLISHER

Thank you for reading this book. If you enjoyed it please do consider leaving a review on Amazon to help others find it too.

We hate typos. All of our books have been rigorously edited and proofread, but sometimes mistakes do slip through. If you have spotted a typo, please do let us know and we can get it amended within hours.

info@bloodhoundbooks.com